THE GENTLE GRAFTER

"*They began to cuss, amiable, and throw down dollars*"

THE GENTLE
GRAFTER

BY

O. HENRY

*Author of " The Four Million," " The Voice of the
City," " The Trimmed Lamp," "Strictly
Business," " Whirligigs," Etc.*

PUBLISHED BY
DOUBLEDAY, PAGE & COMPANY
FOR
REVIEW OF REVIEWS CO.
1917

CONTENTS

THE GENTLE GRAFTER

THE OCTOPUS MAROONED

"**A** TRUST is its weakest point," said Jeff Peters. "That," said I, "sounds like one of those unintelligible remarks such as, 'Why is a policeman?'"

"It is not," said Jeff. "There are no relations between a trust and a policeman. My remark was an epitogram — an axis — a kind of mulct'em in parvo. What it means is that a trust is like an egg, and it is not like an egg. If you want to break an egg you have to do it from the outside. The only way to break up a trust is from the inside. Keep sitting on it until it hatches. Look at the brood of young colleges and libraries that's chirping and peeping all over the country. Yes, sir, every trust bears in its own bosom the seeds of its destruction like a rooster that crows near a Georgia colored Methodist camp meeting, or a Republican announcing himself a candidate for governor of Texas."

I asked Jeff, jestingly, if he had ever, during his checkered, plaided, mottled, pied and dappled career, conducted an enterprise of the class to which the

3

word " trust " had been applied. Somewhat to my surprise he acknowledged the corner.

" Once," said he. " And the state seal of New Jersey never bit into a charter that opened up a solider and safer piece of legitimate octopusing. We had everything in our favor — wind, water, police, nerve, and a clean monopoly of an article indispensable to the public. There wasn't a trust buster on the globe that could have found a weak spot in our scheme. It made Rockefeller's little kerosene speculation look like a bucket shop. But we lost out."

" Some unforeseen opposition came up, I suppose," I said.

" No, sir, it was just as I said. We were self-curbed. It was a case of auto-suppression. There was a rift within the loot, as Albert Tennyson says.

" You remember I told you that me and Andy Tucker was partners for some years. That man was the most talented conniver at stratagems I ever saw. Whenever he saw a dollar in another man's hands he took it as a personal grudge, if he couldn't take it any other way. Andy was educated, too, besides having a lot of useful information. He had acquired a big amount of experience out of books, and could talk for hours on any subject connected with ideas and discourse. He had been in every line of graft from lecturing on Palestine with a lot of magic lantern pictures of the annual Custom-made Clothiers' Association convention at Atlantic City to flooding Connecticut with bogus wood alcohol distilled from nutmegs.

"One Spring me and Andy had been over in Mexico on a flying trip during which a Philadelphia capitalist had paid us $2,500 for a half interest in a silver mine in Chihuahua. Oh, yes, the mine was all right. The other half interest must have been worth two or three hundred thousand. I often wondered who owned that mine.

"In coming back to the United States me and Andy stubbed our toes against a little town in Texas on the bank of the Rio Grande. The name of it was Bird City; but it wasn't. The town had about 2,000 inhabitants, mostly men. I figured out that their principal means of existence was in living close to tall chaparral. Some of 'em were stockmen and some gamblers and some horse peculators and plenty were in the smuggling line. Me and Andy put up at a hotel that was built like something between a roof-garden and a sectional bookcase. It began to rain the day we got there. As the saying is, Juniper Aquarius was sure turning on the water plugs on Mount Amphibious.

"Now, there were three saloons in Bird City, though neither Andy nor me drank. But we could see the townspeople making a triangular procession from one to another all day and half the night. Everybody seemed to know what to do with as much money as they had.

"The third day of the rain it slacked up awhile in the afternoon, so me and Andy walked out to the edge of town to view the mudscape. Bird City was built between the Rio Grande and a deep wide arroyo that used to be the old bed of the river. The bank between the stream and its old bed was cracking and giving away, when we saw it, on account of the high water caused by the rain. Andy looks at it a long time. That man's intellects was never idle. And then he unfolds to me a instantaneous idea that has occurred to him. Right there was organized a trust; and we walked back into town and put it on the market.

"First we went to the main saloon in Bird City, called the Blue Snake, and bought it. It cost us $1,200. And then we dropped in, casual, at Mexican Joe's place, referred to the rain, and bought him out for $500. The other one came easy at $400.

"The next morning Bird City woke up and found itself an island. The river had busted through its old channel, and the town was surrounded by roaring torrents. The rain was still raining, and there was heavy clouds in the northwest that presaged about six more mean annual rainfalls during the next two weeks. But the worst was yet to come.

" Bird City hopped out of its nest, waggled its pin feathers and strolled out for its matutinal toot. Lo! Mexican Joe's place was closed and likewise the other little 'dobe life saving station. So, naturally the body politic emits thirsty ejaculations of surprise and ports hellum for the Blue Snake. And what does it find there?

" Behind one end of the bar sits Jefferson Peters, octopus, with a sixshooter on each side of him, ready to make change or corpses as the case may be. There are three bartenders; and on the wall is a ten foot sign reading: ' All Drinks One Dollar.' Andy sits on the safe in his neat blue suit and gold-banded cigar, on the lookout for emergencies. The town marshal is there with two deputies to keep order, having been promised free drinks by the trust.

" Well, sir, it took Bird City just ten minutes te realize that it was in a cage. We expected trouble; but there wasn't any. The citizens saw that we had 'em. The nearest railroad was thirty miles away; and it would be two weeks at least before the river would

"*They began to cuss, amiable, and throw down dollars.*"

be fordable. So they began to cuss, amiable, and throw down dollars on the bar till it sounded like a selection on the xylophone.

"There was about 1,500 grown-up adults in Bird City that had arrived at years of indiscretion; and the majority of 'em required from three to twenty drinks a day to make life endurable. The Blue Snake was the only place where they could get 'em till the flood subsided. It was beautiful and simple as all truly great swindles are.

"About ten o'clock the silver dollars dropping on the bar slowed down to playing two-steps and marches instead of jigs. But I looked out the windows and saw a hundred or two of our customers standing in line at Bird City Savings and Loan Co., and I knew they were borrowing more money to be sucked in by the clammy tendrils of the octopus.

"At the fashionable hour of noon everybody went home to dinner. We told the bartenders to take advantage of the lull, and do the same. Then me and Andy counted the receipts. We had taken in $1,300. We calculated that if Bird City would only remain an island for two weeks the trust would be able to endow the Chicago University with a new dormitory of padded cells for the faculty, and present every

"*Andy was especial inroaded by self-esteem.*"

worthy poor man in Texas with a farm, provided he
furnished the site for it.

"Andy was especial inroaded by self-esteem at our
success, the rudiments of the scheme having originated
in his own surmises and premonitions. He got off
the safe and lit the biggest cigar in the house.

"'Jeff,' says he, 'I don't suppose that anywhere
in the world you could find three cormorants with
brighter ideas about down-treading the proletariat
than the firm of Peters, Satan and Tucker, incorporated. We have sure handed the small consumer
a giant blow in the sole apopletic region. No?'

"'Well,' says I, 'it does look as if we would have
to take up gastritis and golf or be measured for kilts
in spite of ourselves. This little turn in bug juice is,
verily, all to the Skibo. And I can stand it,' says I.
'I'd rather batten than bant any day.'

"Andy pours himself out four fingers of our best
rye and does with it as was so intended. It was the
first drink I had ever known him to take.

"'By way of liberation,' says he, 'to the gods.'

"And then after thus doing umbrage to the
heathen diabetes he drinks another to our success.
And then he begins to toast the trade, beginning with
Raisuli and the Northern Pacific, and on down the
line to the little ones like the school book combine and

the oleomargarine outrages and the Lehigh Valley and Great Scott Coal Federation.

" ' It's all right, Andy,' says I, ' to drink the health of our brother monopolists, but don't overdo the wassail. You know our most eminent and loathed multi-corruptionists live on weak tea and dog biscuits.'

" Andy went in the back room awhile and came out dressed in his best clothes. There was a kind of murderous and soulful look of gentle riotousness in his eye that I didn't like. I watched him to see what turn the whiskey was going to take in him. There are two times when you never can tell what is going to happen. One is when a man takes his first drink; and the other is when a woman takes her latest.

" In less than an hour Andy's skate had turned to an ice yacht. He was outwardly decent and managed to preserve his aquarium, but inside he was impromptu and full of unexpectedness.

" ' Jeff,' says he, ' do you know that I'm a crater — a living crater?'

" ' That's a self-evident hypothesis,' says I. ' But you're not Irish. Why don't you say ' creature,' according to the rules and syntax of America?'

" ' I'm the crater of a volcano,' says he. ' I'm all aflame and crammed inside with an assortment of words and phrases that have got to have an exodus.

I can feel millions of synonyms and parts of speech rising in me,' says he, ' and I've got to make a speech of some sort. Drink,' says Andy, ' always drives me to oratory.'

" ' It could do no worse,' says I.

" ' From my earliest recollections,' says he, ' alcohol seemed to stimulate my sense of recitation and rhetoric. Why, in Bryan's second campaign,' says Andy, ' they used to give me three gin rickeys and I'd speak two hours longer than Billy himself could on the silver question. Finally they persuaded me to take the gold cure.'

" ' If you've got to get rid of your excess verbiage,' says I, ' why not go out on the river bank and speak a piece? It seems to me there was an old spell-binder named Cantharides that used to go and disincorporate himself of his windy numbers along the seashore.'

" ' No,' says Andy, ' I must have an audience. I feel like if I once turned loose people would begin to call Senator Beveridge the Grand Young Sphinx of the Wabash. I've got to get an audience together, Jeff, and get this oral distension assuaged or it may turn in on me and I'd go about feeling like a deckle-edge edition de luxe of Mrs. E. D. E. N. Southworth.'

" ' On what special subject of the theorems and

topics does your desire for vocality seem to be connected with?' I asks.

"'I ain't particular,' says Andy. 'I am equally good and varicose on all subjects. I can take up the matter of Russian immigration, or the poetry of John W. Keats, or the tariff, or Kabyle literature, or drainage, and make my audience weep, cry, sob and shed tears by turns.'

"'Well, Andy,' says I, 'if you are bound to get rid of this accumulation of vernacular suppose you go out in town and work it on some indulgent citizen. Me and the boys will take care of the business. Everybody will be through dinner pretty soon, and salt pork and beans makes a man pretty thirsty. We ought to take in $1,500 more by midnight.'

" So Andy goes out of the Blue Snake, and I see him stopping men on the street and talking to 'em. By and by he has half a dozen in a bunch listening to him; and pretty soon I see him waving his arms and elocuting at a good-sized crowd on a corner. When he walks away they string out after him, talking all the time; and he leads 'em down the main street of Bird City with more men joining the procession as they go. It reminded me of the old lergendemain that I'd read in books about the Pied Piper of Heidsieck charming the children away from the town.

"And he leads 'em down the main street of Bird City."

" One o'clock came; and then two; and three got under the wire for place; and not a Bird citizen came in for a drink. The streets were deserted except for some ducks and ladies going to the stores. There was only a light drizzle falling then.

" A lonesome man came along and stopped in front of the Blue Snake to scrape the mud off his boots.

" ' Pardner,' says I, ' what has happened? This morning there was hectic gayety afoot; and now it seems more like one of them ruined cities of Tyre and Siphon where the lone lizard crawls on the walls of the main port-cullis.'

" ' The whole town,' says the muddy man, ' is up in Sperry's wool warehouse listening to your side-kicker make a speech. He is some gravy on delivering himself of audible sounds relating to matters and conclusions,' says the man.

" ' Well, I hope he'll adjourn, sine qua non, pretty soon,' says I, ' for trade languishes.'

" Not a customer did we have that afternoon. At six o'clock two Mexicans brought Andy to the saloon lying across the back of a burro. We put him to bed while he still muttered and gesticulated with his hands and feet.

" Then I locked up the cash and went out to see what had happened. I met a man who told me all about it.   Andy had made the finest two hour speech that had ever been heard in Texas, he said, or anywhere else in the world.

"'What was it about?' I asked.

"'Temperance,' says he. 'And when he got through, every man in Bird City signed the pledge for a year.'"

JEFF PETERS AS A PERSONAL MAGNET

JEFF PETERS has been engaged in as many schemes for making money as there are recipes for cooking rice in Charleston, S. C.

Best of all I like to hear him tell of his earlier days when he sold liniments and cough cures on street corners, living hand to mouth, heart to heart with the people, throwing heads or tails with fortune for his last coin.

"I struck Fisher Hill, Arkansaw," said he, "in a buckskin suit, moccasins, long hair and a thirty-carat diamond ring that I got from an actor in Texarkana. I don't know what he ever did with the pocket knife I swapped him for it.

"I was Dr. Waugh-hoo, the celebrated Indian medicine man. I carried only one best bet just then, and that was Resurrection Bitters. It was made of life-giving plants and herbs accidentally discovered by Ta-qua-la, the beautiful wife of the chief of the Choctaw Nation, while gathering truck to garnish a platter of boiled dog for the annual corn dance.

"Business hadn't been good at the last town, so I

18

" Life began to look rosy again."

only had five dollars. I went to the Fisher Hill druggist and he credited me for half a gross of eight-ounce bottles and corks. I had the labels and ingredients in my valise, left over from the last town. Life began to look rosy again after I got in my hotel room with the water running from the tap, and the Resurrection Bitters lining up on the table by the dozen.

"Fake? No, sir. There was two dollars' worth of fluid extract of cinchona and a dime's worth of aniline in that half-gross of bitters. I've gone through towns years afterwards and had folks ask for 'em again.

"I hired a wagon that night and commenced selling the bitters on Main Street. Fisher Hill was a low, malarial town; and a compound hypothetical pneumo-cardiac anti-scorbutic tonic was just what I diagnosed the crowd as needing. The bitters started off like sweetbreads-on-toast at a vegetarian dinner. I had sold two dozen at fifty cents apiece when I felt somebody pull my coat tail. I knew what that meant; so I climbed down and sneaked a five dollar bill into the hand of a man with a German silver star on his lapel.

"'Constable,' says I, 'it's a fine night.'

"'Have you got a city license,' he asks, 'to sell this illegitimate essence of spooju that you flatter by the name of medicine?'

" ' I have not,' says I. ' I didn't know you had a city. If I can find it to-morrow I'll take one out if it's necessary.'

" 'I commenced selling the bitters on Main Street."

" ' I'll have to close you up till you do,' says the constable.

" I quit selling and went back to the hotel. I was talking to the landlord about it.

" ' Oh, you won't stand no show in Fisher Hill,' says he. ' Dr. Hoskins, the only doctor here, is a brother-in-law of the Mayor, and they won't allow no fake doctor to practice in town.'

" ' I don't practice medicine,' says I, ' I've got a State peddler's license, and I take out a city one wherever they demand it.'

" I went to the Mayor's office the next morning and they told me he hadn't showed up yet. They didn't know when he'd be down. So Doc Waugh-hoo hunches down again in a hotel chair and lights a jimpson-weed regalia, and waits.

" By and by a young man in a blue necktie slips into the chair next to me and asks the time.

" ' Half-past ten,' says I, ' and you are Andy Tucker. I've seen you work. Wasn't it you that put up the Great Cupid Combination package on the Southern States? Let's see, it was a Chilian diamond engagement ring, a wedding ring, a potato masher, a bottle of soothing syrup and Dorothy Vernon — all for fifty cents.'

" Andy was pleased to hear that I remembered him. He was a good street man; and he was more than that — he respected his profession, and he was satisfied with 300 per cent. profit. He had plenty of offers to go into the illegitimate drug and garden seed business; but he was never to be tempted off of the straight path.

"I wanted a partner, so Andy and me agreed to go out together. I told him about the situation in Fisher Hill and how finances was low on account of the local mixture of politics and jalap. Andy had just got in on the train that morning. He was pretty low himself, and was going to canvass the town for a few dollars to build a new battleship by popular subscription at Eureka Springs. So we went out and sat on the porch and talked it over.

"The next morning at eleven o'clock when I was sitting there alone, an Uncle Tom shuffles into the hotel and asked for the doctor to come and see Judge Banks, who, it seems, was the mayor and a mighty sick man.

"'I'm no doctor,' says I. 'Why don't you go and get the doctor?'

"'Boss,' says he, 'Doc Hoskins am done gone twenty miles in de country to see some sick persons. He's de only doctor in de town, and Massa Banks am powerful bad off. He sent me to ax you to please, suh, come.'

"'As man to man,' says I, 'I'll go and look him over.' So I put a bottle of Resurrection Bitters in my pocket and goes up on the hill to the mayor's mansion, the finest house in town, with a mansard roof and two cast iron dogs on the lawn.

"This Mayor Banks was in bed all but his whiskers and feet. He was making internal noises that would have had everybody in San Francisco hiking for the parks. A young man was standing by the bed holding a cup of water.

"'Doc,' says the Mayor, 'I'm awful sick. I'm about to die. Can't you do nothing for me?'

"'Mr. Mayor,' says I, 'I'm not a regular preordained disciple of S. Q. Lapius. I never took a course in a medical college,' says I. 'I've just come as a fellow man to see if I could be of assistance.'

"'I'm deeply obliged,' says he. 'Doc Waughhoo, this is my nephew, Mr. Biddle. He has tried to alleviate my distress, but without success. Oh, Lordy! Ow-ow-ow!!' he sings out.

"I nods at Mr. Biddle and sets down by the bed and feels the mayor's pulse. 'Let me see your liver — your tongue, I mean,' says I. Then I turns up the lids of his eyes and looks close at the pupils of 'em.

"'How long have you been sick?' I asked.

"'I was taken down — ow-ouch — last night,' says the Mayor. 'Gimme something for it, doc, won't you?'

"'Mr. Fiddle,' says I, 'raise the window shade a bit, will you?'

"'Biddle,' says the young man. 'Do you feel like you could eat some ham and eggs, Uncle James?'

"'Mr. Mayor,' says I, after laying my ear to his right shoulder blade and listening, 'you've got a bad attack of super-inflammation of the right clavicle of the harpsichord!'

"'Good Lord!' says he, with a groan, 'Can't you rub something on it, or set it or anything?'

"I picks up my hat and starts for the door.

"'You ain't going, doc?' says the Mayor with a howl. 'You ain't going away and leave me to die with this — superfluity of the clapboards, are you?'

"'Common humanity, Dr. Whoa-ha,' says Mr. Biddle, 'ought to prevent your deserting a fellow-human in distress.'

"'Dr. Waugh-hoo, when you get through plowing,' says I. And then I walks back to the bed and throws back my long hair.

"'Mr. Mayor,' says I, 'there is only one hope for you. Drugs will do you no good. But there is another power higher yet, although drugs are high enough,' says I.

"'And what is that?' says he.

"'Scientific demonstrations,' says I. 'The

triumph of mind over sarsaparilla. The belief that there is no pain and sickness except what is produced when we ain't feeling well. Declare yourself in arrears. Demonstrate.'

" ' What is this paraphernalia you speak of, Doc? ' says the Mayor. ' You ain't a Socialist, are you? '

" ' I am speaking,' says I, ' of the great doctrine of psychic financiering — of the enlightened school of long-distance, sub-conscientious treatment of fallacies and meningitis — of that wonderful in-door sport known as personal magnetism.'

" ' Can you work it, doc? ' asks the Mayor.

" ' I'm one of the Sole Sanhedrims and Ostensible Hooplas of the Inner Pulpit,' says I. ' The lame talk and the blind rubber whenever I make a pass at 'em. I am a medium, a coloratura hypnotist and a spirituous control. It was only through me at the recent seances at Ann Arbor that the late president of the Vinegar Bitters Company could revisit the earth to communicate with his sister Jane. You see me peddling medicine on the streets,' says I, ' to the poor. I don't practice personal magnetism on them. I do not drag it in the dust,' says I, ' because they haven't got the dust.'

" ' Will you treat my case? ' asks the Mayor.

" ' Listen,' says I. ' I've had a good deal of

trouble with medical societies everywhere I've been. I don't practice medicine. But, to save your life, I'll give you the psychic treatment if you'll agree as mayor not to push the license question.'

" ' Of course I will,' says he. ' And now get to work, doc, for them pains are coming on again.'

" ' My fee will be $250.00, cure guaranteed in two treatments,' says I.

" ' All right,' says the Mayor. ' I'll pay it. I guess my life's worth that much.'

" I sat down by the bed and looked him straight in the eye.

" ' Now,' says I, ' get your mind off the disease. You ain't sick. You haven't got a heart or a clavicle or a funny bone or brains or anything. You haven't got any pain. Declare error. Now you feel the pain that you didn't have leaving, don't you? '

" ' I do feel some little better, doc,' says the Mayor, ' darned if I don't. Now state a few lies about my not having this swelling in my left side, and I think I could be propped up and have some sausage and buckwheat cakes.'

" I made a few passes with my hands.

" ' Now,' says I, ' the inflammation's gone. The right lobe of the perihelion has subsided. You're getting sleepy. You can't hold your eyes open any

longer. For the present the disease is checked. **Now,**
you are asleep.'

" The Mayor shut his eyes slowly and began to
snore.

" ' You observe, Mr. Tiddle,' says I, ' the wonders
of modern science.'

" ' Biddle,' says he, ' When will you give uncle the
rest of the treatment, Dr. Pooh-pooh? '

" ' Waugh-hoo,' says I. ' I'll come back at eleven
to-morrow. When he wakes up give him eight drops
of turpentine and three pounds of steak. Good morning.'

" The next morning I went back on time. ' Well,
Mr. Riddle,' says I, when he opened the bedroom
door, ' and how is uncle this morning? '

" ' He seems much better,' says the young man.

" The mayor's color and pulse was fine. I gave him
another treatment, and he said the last of the pain
left him.

" ' Now,' says I, ' you'd better stay in bed for a
day or two, and you'll be all right. It's a good thing
I happened to be in Fisher Hill, Mr. Mayor,' says
I, ' for all the remedies in the cornucopia that the regular schools of medicine use couldn't have saved you.
And now that error has flew and pain proved a per-
jurer, let's allude to a cheerfuller subject — say the

fee of $250.   No checks, please, I hate to write my
name on the back of a check almost as bad as I do on
the front.'

" ' I've got the cash here,' says the mayor, pulling
a pocket book from under his pillow.

" He counts out five fifty-dollar notes and holds
'em in his hand.

" ' Bring the receipt,' he says to Biddle.

" I signed the receipt and the mayor handed me
the money.   I put it in my inside pocket careful.

" ' Now do your duty officer,' says the mayor grin-
ning much unlike a sick man.

" Mr. Biddle lays his hand on my arm.

" ' You're under arrest, Dr. Waugh-hoo, alias
Peters,' says he, ' for practising medicine without au-
thority under the State law.'

" ' Who are you? ' I asks.

" ' I'll tell you who he is,' says Mr. Mayor, sitting
up in bed.   ' He's a detective employed by the State
Medical Society.   He's been following you over five
counties.   He came to me yesterday and we fixed up
this scheme to catch you.   I guess you won't do any
more doctoring around these parts, Mr. Fakir.   What
was it you said I had, doc? ' the mayor laughs, ' compound — well it wasn't softening of the brain, I
guess, anyway.'

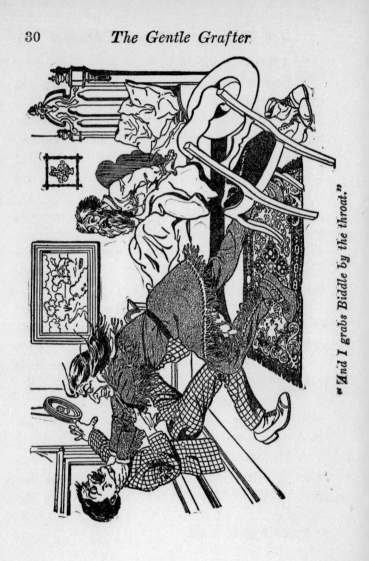

"*And I grabs Biddle by the throat.*"

" ' A detective,' says I.

" ' Correct,' says Biddle. ' I'll have to turn you over to the sheriff.'

" ' Let's see you do it,' says I, and I grabs Biddle by the throat and half throws him out the window, but he pulls a gun and sticks it under my chin, and I stand still. Then he puts handcuffs on me, and takes the money out of my pocket.

" ' I witness,' says he, ' that they're the same bills that you and I marked, Judge Banks. I'll turn them over to the sheriff when we get to his office, and he'll send you a receipt. They'll have to be used as evidence in the case.'

" ' All right, Mr. Biddle,' says the mayor. ' And now, Doc Waugh-hoo,' he goes on, ' why don't you demonstrate? Can't you pull the cork out of your magnetism with your teeth and hocus-pocus them handcuffs off? '

" ' Come on, officer,' says I, dignified. ' I may as well make the best of it.' And then I turns to old Banks and rattles my chains.

" ' Mr. Mayor,' says I, ' the time will come soon when you'll believe that personal magnetism is a success. And you'll be sure that it succeeded in this case, too.'

" And I guess it did.

"When we got nearly to the gate, I says: 'We might meet somebody now, Andy. I reckon you better take 'em off, and —' Hey? Why, of course it was Andy Tucker. That was his scheme; and that's how we got the capital to go into business together."

MODERN RURAL SPORTS

JEFF PETERS must be reminded. Whenever he is called upon, pointedly, for a story, he will maintain that his life has been as devoid of incident as the longest of Trollope's novels. But lured, he will divulge. Therefore I cast many and divers flies upon the current of his thoughts before I feel a nibble.

" I notice," said I, " that the Western farmers, in spite of their prosperity, are running after their old populistic idols again."

" It's the running season," said Jeff, " for farmers, shad, maple trees and the Connemaugh river. I know something about farmers. I thought I struck one once that had got out of the rut; but Andy Tucker proved to me I was mistaken. 'Once a farmer, always a sucker,' said Andy. 'He's the man that's shoved into the front row among bullets, ballots and the ballet. He's the funny-bone and gristle of the country,' said Andy, 'and I don't know who we would do without him.'

" One morning me and Andy wakes up with sixty-eight cents between us in a yellow pine hotel on the edge of the pre-digested hoe-cake belt of Southern Indiana. How we got off the train there the night before I can't tell you; for she went through the village so fast that what looked like a saloon to us through the car window turned out to be a composite view of a drug store and a water tank two blocks apart. Why we got off at the first station we could, belongs to a little oroide gold watch and Alaska diamond deal we failed to pull off the day before, over the Kentucky line.

"When I woke up I heard roosters crowing, and smelt something like the fumes of nitro-muriatic acid, and heard something heavy fall on the floor below us, and a man swearing.

"'Cheer up, Andy,' says I. 'We're in a rural community. Somebody has just tested a gold brick downstairs. We'll go out and get what's coming to us from a farmer; and then yoicks! and away.'

"Farmers was always a kind of reserve fund to me. Whenever I was in hard luck I'd go to the crossroads, hook a finger in a farmer's suspender, recite the prospectus of my swindle in a mechanical kind of a way, look over what he had, give him back his keys, whetstone and papers that was of no value except to owner, and stroll away without asking any questions.

Farmers are not fair game to me as high up in our business as me and Andy was; but there was times when we found 'em useful, just as Wall Street does the Secretary of the Treasury now and then.

" When we went down stairs we saw we was in the midst of the finest farming section we ever see. About two miles away on a hill was a big white house in a grove surrounded by a wide-spread agricultural agglomeration of fields and barns and pastures and out-houses.

" ' Whose house is that? ' we asked the landlord.

" ' That,' says he, ' is the domicile and the arboreal, terrestrial and horticultural accessories of Farmer Ezra Plunkett, one of our county's most progressive citizens.'

" After breakfast me and Andy, with eight cents capital left, casts the horoscope of the rural potentate.

" ' Let me go alone,' says I. ' Two of us against one farmer would look as one-sided as Roosevelt using both hands to kill a grizzly.'

" ' All right,' says Andy. ' I like to be a true sport even when I'm only collecting rebates from the ruta-bag raisers. What bait are you going to use for this Ezra thing? ' Andy asks me.

" ' Oh,' says I, ' the first thing that come to hand in the suit case. I reckon I'll take along some of the new income tax receipts; and the recipe for making clover honey out of clabber and apple peelings; and the order blanks for the McGuffey's readers, which afterwards turn out to be McCormick reapers; and the pearl necklace found on the train; and a pocket-size goldbrick; and a —'

" ' That'll be enough,' says Andy. ' Any one of the lot ought to land on Ezra. And, say, Jeff, make that succotash fancier give you nice, clean, new bills. It's a disgrace to our Department of Agriculture, Civil Service and Pure Food Law the kind of stuff some of these farmers hand out to us. I've had to take rolls from 'em that looked like bundles of microbe cultures captured out of a Red Cross ambulance.'

" So, I goes to a livery stable and hires a buggy on my looks. I drove out to the Plunkett farm and hitched. There was a man sitting on the front steps of the house. He had on a white flannel suit, a diamond ring, golf cap and a pink ascot tie. ' Summer boarder,' says I to myself.

" ' I'd like to see Farmer Ezra Plunkett,' says I to him.

" ' You see him,' says he. ' What seems to be on your mind?'

" I never answered a word. I stood still, repeating

to myself the rollicking lines of that merry jingle,
' The Man with the Hoe.' When I looked at this
farmer, the little devices I had in my pocket for
buncoing the pushed-back brows seemed as hopeless
as trying to shake down the Beef Trust with a mitti-
mus and a parlor rifle.

" ' Well,' says he, looking at me close, ' speak up.
I see the left pocket of your coat sags a good deal.
Out with the goldbrick first. I'm rather more interested in the bricks than I am in the trick sixty-day
notes and the lost silver mine story.'

" I had a kind of cerebral sensation of foolishness
in my ideas of ratiocination; but I pulled out the little
brick and unwrapped my handkerchief off it.

" ' One dollar and eighty cents,' says the farmer
hefting it in his hand. ' Is it a trade? '

" ' The lead in it is worth more than that,' says I,
dignified. I put it back in my pocket.

" ' All right,' says he. ' But I sort of wanted it
for the collection I'm starting. I got a $5,000 one
last week for $2.10.'

" Just then a telephone bell rings in the house.

" ' Come in, Bunk,' says the farmer, ' and look at
my place. It's kind of lonesome here sometimes. I
think that's New York calling.'

" We went inside. The room looked like a Broadway stockbroker's — light-oak desks, two 'phones, Spanish leather upholstered chairs and couches, oil paintings in gilt frames a foot deep and a ticker hitting off the news in one corner.

" ' Hello, hello ! ' says this funny farmer. ' Is that the Regent Theatre? Yes; this is Plunkett, of Woodbine Centre. Reserve four orchestra seats for Friday evening — my usual ones. Yes; Friday — good-bye.'

" ' I run over to New York every two weeks to see a show,' says the farmer, hanging up the receiver. ' I catch the eighteen-hour flyer at Indianapolis, spend ten hours in the heyday of night on the Yappian Way, and get home in time to see the chickens go to roost forty-eight hours later. Oh, the pristine Hubbard squasherino of the cave-dwelling period is getting geared up some for the annual meeting of the Don't-Blow-Out-the-Gas Association, don't you think, Mr. Bunk? '

" ' I seem to perceive,' says I, ' a kind of hiatus in the agrarian traditions in which heretofore, I have reposed confidence.'

" ' Sure, Bunk,' says he. ' The yellow primrose on the river's brim is getting to look to us Reubs like a holiday edition de luxe of the Language of Flowers with deckle edges and frontispiece.'

" Just then the telephone calls him again.

" ' Hello, hello! ' says he. ' Oh, that's Perkins, at Milldale. I told you $800 was too much for that horse. Have you got him there? Good. Let me see him. Get away from the transmitter. Now make him trot in a circle. Faster. Yes, I can hear him. Keep on — faster yet. . . . That'll do. Now lead him up to the phone. Closer. Get his nose nearer. There. Now wait. No; I don't want that horse. What? No; not at any price. He interferes; and he's windbroken. Goodbye.'

" ' Now, Bunk,' says the farmer, ' do you begin to realize that agriculture has had a hair cut? You belong in a bygone era. Why, Tom Lawson himself knows better than to try to catch an up-to-date agriculturist napping. It's Saturday, the Fourteenth, on the farm, you bet. Now, look here, and see how we keep up with the day's doings.'

" He shows me a machine on a table with two things for your ears like the penny-in-the-slot affairs. I puts it on and listens. A female voice starts up reading headlines of murders, accidents and other political casualities.

" ' What you hear,' says the farmer, ' is a synopsis of to-day's news in the New York, Chicago, St. Louis and San Francisco papers. It is wired in to our Rural News Bureau and served hot to subscribers.

On this table you see the principal dailies and weeklies of the country. Also a special service of advance sheets of the monthly magazines.'

" I picks up one sheet and sees that it's headed: ' Special Advance Proofs. In July, 1909, the *Century* will say '— and so forth.

" The farmer rings up somebody — his manager, I reckon — and tells him to let that herd of 15 Jerseys go at $600 a head; and to sow the 900-acre field in wheat; and to have 200 extra cans ready at the station for the milk trolley car. Then he passes the Henry Clays and sets out a bottle of green chartreuse, and goes over and looks at the ticker tape.

" ' Consolidated Gas up two points,' says he. ' Oh, very well.'

" ' Ever monkey with copper? ' I asks.

" ' Stand back! ' says he, raising his hand, ' or I'll call the dog. I told you not to waste your time.'

" After a while he says: ' Bunk, if you don't mind my telling you, your company begins to cloy slightly. I've got to write an article on the Chimera of Communism for a magazine, and attend a meeting of the Race Track Association this afternoon. Of course you understand by now that you can't get my proxy for your Remedy, whatever it may be.'

" Well, sir, all I could think of to do was to go

out and get in the buggy. The horse turned round and took me back to the hotel. I hitched him and went in to see Andy. In his room I told him about this farmer, word for word; and I sat picking at the table cover like one bereft of sagaciousness.

"'I don't understand it,' says I, humming a sad and foolish little song to cover my humiliation.

"Andy walks up and down the room for a long time, biting the left end of his mustache as he does when in the act of thinking.

"'Jeff,' says he, finally, 'I believe your story of this expurgated rustic; but I am not convinced. It looks incredulous to me that he could have inoculated himself against all the preordained systems of bucolic bunco. Now, you never regarded me as a man of special religious proclivities, did you, Jeff?' says Andy.

"'Well,' says I, 'No. But,' says I, not to wound his feelings, 'I have also observed many church members whose said proclivities were not so outwardly developed that they would show on a white handkerchief if you rubbed 'em with it.'

"'I have always been a deep student of nature from creation down,' says Andy, 'and I believe in an ultimatum design of Providence. Farmers was made for a purpose; and that was to furnish a livelihood to men like me and you. Else why was we given brains? It is my belief that the manna that the Is-raelites lived on for forty years in the wilderness was only a figurative word for farmers; and they kept up the practice to this day. And now,' says Andy, 'I am going to test my theory "Once a farmer, always a come-on," in spite of the veneering and the orifices that a spurious civilization has brought to him.'

"'You'll fail, same as I did,' says I. 'This one's shook off the shackles of the sheep-fold. He's en-trenched behind the advantages of electricity, educa-tion, literature and intelligence.'

"'I'll try,' said Andy. 'There are certain Laws of Nature that Free Rural Delivery can't overcome.'

"Andy fumbles around awhile in the closet and comes out dressed in a suit with brown and yellow checks as big as your hand. His vest is red with blue dots, and he wears a high silk hat. I noticed he'd soaked his sandy mustache in a kind of blue ink.

"'Great Barnums?' says I. 'You're a ringer for a circus thimblerig man.'

"'Right,' says Andy. 'Is the buggy outside? Wait here till I come back. I won't be long.'

"Two hours afterwards Andy steps in the room and lays a wad of money on the table.

"'Eight hundred and sixty dollars,' said he. 'Let

me tell you. He was in. He looked me over and began to guy me. I didn't say a word, but got out the walnut shells and began to roll the little ball on the table. I whistled a tune or two, and then I started up the old formula.

" 'Step up lively, gentlemen,' says I, ' and watch the little ball. It costs you nothing to look. There you see it, and there you don't. Guess where the little joker is. The quickness of the hand deceives the eye.'

" ' I steals a look at the farmer man. I see the sweat coming out on his forehead. He goes over and closes the front door and watches me some more. Directly he says: " I'll bet you twenty I can pick the shell the ball's under now."

" ' After that,' goes on Andy, ' there is nothing new to relate. He only had $860 in cash in the house. When I left he followed me to the gate. There was tears in his eyes when he shook hands.

" ' " Bunk," ' says he, ' " thank you for the only real pleasure I've had in years. It brings up happy old days when I was only a farmer and not an agriculturist. God bless you." ' "

Here Jeff Peters ceased, and I inferred that his story was done.

" Then you think "— I began.

" Yes," said Jeff.   " Something like that.   You let the farmers go ahead and amuse themselves with politics.   Farming's a lonesome life; and they've been against the shell game before."

THE CHAIR OF PHILANTHROMATHE-
MATICS

"I SEE that the cause of Education has received the princely gift of more than fifty millions of dollars," said I.

I was gleaning the stray items from the evening papers while Jeff Peters packed his briar pipe with plug cut.

"Which same," said Jeff, "calls for a new deck, and a recitation by the entire class in philanthromathematics."

"Is that an allusion?" I asked.

"It is," said Jeff. "I never told you about the time when me and Andy Tucker was philanthropists, did I? It was eight years ago in Arizona. Andy and me was out in the Gila mountains with a two-horse wagon prospecting for silver. We struck it, and sold out to parties in Tucson for $25,000. They paid our check at the bank in silver — a thousand dollars in a sack. We loaded it in our wagon and drove east a hundred miles before we recovered our presence of intellect. Twenty-five thousand dollars don't sound like so much when you're reading the annual report of the Pennsylvania Railroad or listening to an actor talking about his salary; but when you can raise up a wagon sheet and kick around with your bootheel and hear every one of 'em ring against another it makes you feel like you was a night-and-day bank with the clock striking twelve.

" The third day out we drove into one of the most specious and tidy little towns that Nature or Rand and McNally ever turned out. It was in the foot-hills, and mitigated with trees and flowers and about 2,000 head of cordial and dilatory inhabitants. The town seemed to be called Floresville, and Nature had not contaminated it with many railroads, fleas or Eastern tourists.

" Me and Andy deposited our money to the credit of Peters and Tucker in the Esperanza Savings Bank, and got rooms at the Skyview Hotel. After supper we lit up, and sat out on the gallery and smoked. Then was when the philanthropy idea struck me. I suppose every grafter gets it sometime.

" When a man swindles the public out of a certain amount he begins to get scared and wants to return part of it. And if you'll watch close and notice the way his charity runs you'll see that he tries to restore it to the same people he got it from. As a hydrostatical case, take, let's say, A. A made his millions selling oil to poor students who sit up nights studying political economy and methods for regulating the trusts. So, back to the universities and colleges goes his conscience dollars.

" There's B got his from the common laboring man that works with his hands and tools. How's he to get some of the remorse fund back into their overalls?

" ' Aha!' says B, ' I'll do it in the name of Education. I've skinned the laboring man,' says he to himself, ' but, according to the old proverb, " Charity covers a multitude of skins." '

" So he puts up eighty million dollars' worth of libraries; and the boys with the dinner pail that builds 'em gets the benefit.

" ' Where's the books? ' asks the reading public.

" ' I dinna ken,' says B. ' I offered ye libraries; and there they are. I suppose if I'd given ye preferred steel trust stock instead ye'd have wanted the water in it set out in cut glass decanters. Hoot, for ye!'

" But, as I said, the owning of so much money was

beginning to give me philanthropitis. It was the first time me and Andy had ever made a pile big enough to make us stop and think how we got it.

" ' Andy,' says I, ' we're wealthy — not beyond the dreams of average; but in our humble way we are comparatively as rich as Greasers. I feel as if I'd like to do something for as well as to humanity.'

" ' I was thinking the same thing, Jeff,' says he. ' We've been gouging the public for a long time with all kinds of little schemes from selling self-igniting celluloid collars to flooding Georgia with Hoke Smith presidential campaign buttons. I'd like, myself, to hedge a bet or two in the graft game if I could do it without actually banging the cymbalines in the Salvation Army or teaching a bible class by the Bertillon system.'

" ' What'll we do? ' says Andy. ' Give free grub to the poor or send a couple of thousand to George Cortelyou? '

" ' Neither,' says I. ' We've got too much money to be implicated in plain charity; and we haven't got enough to make restitution. So, we'll look about for something that's about half way between the two.'

" The next day in walking around Floresville we see on a hill a big red brick building that appears to be disinhabited. The citizens speak up and tell us

that it was begun for a residence several years before
by a mine owner. 'After running up the house he
finds he only had $2.80 left to furnish it with, so he
invests that in whiskey and jumps off the roof on a
spot where he now requiescats in pieces.

"As soon as me and Andy saw that building the
same idea struck both of us. We would fix it up with
lights and pen wipers and professors, and put an iron
dog and statues of Hercules and Father John on the
lawn, and start one of the finest free educational
institutions in the world right there.

"So we talks it over to the prominent citizens of
Floresville, who falls in fine with the idea. They give
a banquet in the engine house to us, and we make our
bow for the first time as benefactors to the cause of
progress and enlightenment. 'Andy makes an hour-
and-a-half speech on the subject of irrigation in
Lower Egypt, and we have a moral tune on the phon-
ograph and pineapple sherbet.

"Andy and me didn't lose any time in philan-
thropping. We put every man in town that could
tell a hammer from a step ladder to work on the
building, dividing it up into class rooms and lecture
halls. We wire to Frisco for a car load of desks,
footballs, arithmetics, penholders, dictionaries, chairs
for the professors, slates, skeletons, sponges, twenty-

seven cravenetted gowns and caps for the senior class, and an open order for all the truck that goes with a first-class university. I took it on myself to put a campus and a curriculum on the list; but the telegraph operator must have got the words wrong, being an ignorant man, for when the goods come we found a can of peas and a curry-comb among 'em.

" While the weekly papers was having chalk-plate cuts of me and Andy we wired an employment agency in Chicago to express us f. o. b., six professors immediately — one English literature, one up-to-date dead languages, one chemistry, one political economy — democrat preferred —one logic, and one wise to painting, Italian and music, with union card. The Esperanza bank guaranteeed salaries, which was to run between $800 and $800.50.

" Well, sir, we finally got in shape. Over the front door was carved the words: ' The World's University; Peters & Tucker, Patrons and Proprietors.' And when September the first got a cross-mark on the calendar, the come-ons begun to roll in. First the faculty got off the tri-weekly express from Tucson. They was mostly young, spectacled and red-headed, with sentiments divided between ambition and food. Andy and me got 'em billeted on the Floresvillians and then laid for the students.

"They came in bunches. We had advertised the University in all the state papers, and it did us good to see how quick the country responded. Two hundred and nineteen husky lads aging along from 18 up to chin whiskers answered the clarion call of free education. They ripped open that town, sponged the seams, turned it, lined it with new mohair; and you couldn't have told it from Harvard or Goldfields at the March term of court.

"They marched up and down the streets waving flags with the World's University colors — ultramarine and blue — and they certainly made a lively place of Floresville. Andy made them a speech from the balcony of the Skyview Hotel, and the whole town was out celebrating.

"In about two weeks the professors got the students disarmed and herded into classes. I don't believe there's any pleasure equal to being a philanthropist. Me and Andy bought high silk hats and pretended to dodge the two reporters of the Floresville Gazette. The paper had a man to kodak us whenever we appeared on the street, and ran our pictures every week over the column headed 'Educational Notes.' Andy lectured twice a week at the University; and afterward I would rise and tell a humorous story. Once the Gazette printed my pictures with Abe Lincoln on one side and Marshall P. Wilder on the other.

" Andy was as interested in philanthropy as I was.
We used to wake up of nights and tell each other new
ideas for booming the University.

" ' Andy,' says I to him one day, ' there's something we overlooked.　The boys ought to have dromedaries.'

" ' What's that?' Andy asks.

" ' Why, something to sleep in, of course,' says I.
' All colleges have 'em.'

" ' Oh, you mean pajamas,' says Andy.

" ' I do not,' says I.　' I mean dromedaries.'　But
I never could make Andy understand; so we never
ordered 'em.　Of course, I meant them long bed-
rooms in colleges where the scholars sleep in a row.

" Well, sir, the World's University was a success.
We had scholars from five States and territories, and
Floresville had a boom.　'A new shooting gallery and
a pawn shop and two more saloons started; and the
boys got up a college yell that went this way:

> " ' Raw, raw, raw,
> 　　Done, done, done,
> 　Peters, Tucker,
> 　Lots of fun.
> 　Bow-wow-wow,
> 　Haw-hee-haw,
> 　World University,
> 　　Hip, hurrah!' "

" The scholars was a fine lot of young men, and me and Andy was as proud of 'em as if they belonged to our own family.

" But one day about the last of October Andy come to me and asks if I have any idea how much money we had left in the bank. I guesses about sixteen thousand. 'Our balance,' says Andy, 'is $821.62.'

" ' What!' says I, with a kind of a yell. 'Do you mean to tell me that them infernal clod-hopping, dough-headed, pup-faced, goose-brained, gate-stealing, rabbit-eared sons of horse thieves have soaked us for that much?'

" ' No less,' says Andy.

" ' Then, to Helvetia with philanthropy,' says I.

" ' Not necessarily,' says Andy. 'Philanthropy,' says he, 'when run on a good business basis is one of the best grafts going. I'll look into the matter and see if it can't be straightened out.'

" The next week I am looking over the payroll of our faculty when I run across a new name — Professor James Darnley McCorkle, chair of mathematics; salary $100 per week. I yells so loud that Andy runs in quick.

" ' What's this,' says I. 'A professor of mathematics at more than $5,000 a year? How did this happen? Did he get in through the window and appoint himself?'

"'I wired to Frisco for him a week ago,' says Andy. 'In ordering the faculty we seemed to have overlooked the chair of mathematics.'

"'A good thing we did,' says I. 'We can pay his salary two weeks, and then our philanthropy will look like the ninth hole on the Skibo golf links.'

"'Wait a while,' says Andy, 'and see how things turn out. We have taken up too noble a cause to draw out now. Besides, the further I gaze into the retail philanthropy business the better it looks to me. I never thought about investigating it before. Come to think of it now,' goes on Andy, 'all the philanthropists I ever knew had plenty of money. I ought to have looked into that matter long ago, and located which was the cause and which was the effect.'

"'I had confidence in Andy's chicanery in financial affairs, so I left the whole thing in his hands. The University was flourishing fine, and me and Andy kept our silk hats shined up, and Floresville kept on heaping honors on us like we was millionaires instead of almost busted philanthropists.

"The students kept the town lively and prosperous. Some stranger came to town and started a faro bank over the Red Front livery stable, and began to amass money in quantities. Me and Andy strolled up one night and piked a dollar or two for sociability. There were about fifty of our students there drinking rum punches and shoving high stacks of blues and reds about the table as the dealer turned the cards up.

" ' Why, dang it, Andy,' says I, ' these free-school-hunting, gander-headed, silk-socked little sons of sap-suckers have got more money than you and me ever had. Look at the rolls they're pulling out of their pistol pockets? '

" ' Yes,' says Andy, ' a good many of them are sons of wealthy miners and stockmen. It's very sad to see 'em wasting their opportunities this way.'

" At Christmas all the students went home to spend the holidays. We had a farewell blowout at the University, and Andy lectured on ' Modern Music and Prehistoric Literature of the Archipelagos.' Each one of the faculty answered to toasts, and compared me and Andy to Rockefeller and the Emperor Marcus Autolycus. I pounded on the table and yelled for Professor McCorkle; but it seems he wasn't present on the occasion. I wanted a look at the man that Andy thought could earn $100 a week in philanthropy that was on the point of making an assignment.

"The students all left on the night train; and the town sounded as quiet as the campus of a correspondence school at midnight. When I went to the hotel I saw a light in Andy's room, and I opened the door and walked in.

"There sat Andy and the faro dealer at a table dividing a two-foot high stack of currency in thousand-dollar packages.

"'Correct,' says Andy. 'Thirty-one thousand apiece. Come in, Jeff,' says he. 'This is our share of the profits of the first half of the scholastic term of the World's University, incorporated and philanthropated. Are you convinced now,' says Andy, 'that philanthropy when practiced in a business way is an art that blesses him who gives as well as him who receives?'

"'Great!' says I, feeling fine. 'I'll admit you are the doctor this time.'

"'We'll be leaving on the morning train,' says Andy. 'You'd better get your collars and cuffs and press clippings together.'

"'Great!' says I. 'I'll be ready. But, Andy,' says I, 'I wish I could have met that Professor James Darnley McCorkle before we went. I had a curiosity to know that man.'

" ' That'll be easy,' says Andy, turning around to the faro dealer.

" ' Jim,' says Andy, ' shake hands with Mr. Peters.' "

THE HAND THAT RILES THE WORLD

"MANY of our great men," said I (apropos of many things), "have declared that they owe their success to the aid and encouragement of some brilliant woman."

"I know," said Jeff Peters. "I've read in history and mythology about Joan of Arc and Mme. Yale and Mrs. Caudle and Eve and other noted females of the past. But, in my opinion, the woman of to-day is of little use in politics or business. What's she best in, anyway? — men make the best cooks, milliners, nurses, housekeepers, stenographers, clerks, hairdressers and launderers. About the only job left that a woman can beat a man in is female impersonator in vaudeville.

"I would have thought," said I, "that occasionally, anyhow, you would have found the wit and intuition of woman valuable to you in your lines of-er-business."

"Now, wouldn't you," said Jeff, with an emphatic nod — "wouldn't you have imagined that? But a woman is an absolutely unreliable partner in any

"*Selling walking canes.*"

straight swindle.   She's liable to turn honest on you
when you are depending upon her the most.   I tried
'em once."

   " Bill Humble, an old friend of mine in the Territories, conceived the illusion that he wanted to be appointed United States Marshal.   At that time me
and Andy was doing a square, legitimate business of
selling walking canes.   If you unscrewed the head
of one and turned it up to your mouth a half pint of
good rye whiskey would go trickling down your
throat to reward you for your act of intelligence.
The deputies was annoying me and Andy some, and
when Bill spoke to me about his officious aspirations,
I saw how the appointment as Marshal might help
along the firm of Peters & Tucker.

   " ' Jeff,' says Bill to me, ' you are a man of learning and education, besides having knowledge and information concerning not only rudiments but facts
and attainments.'

   " ' I do so,' says I, ' and I have never regretted it.
I am not one,' says I, ' who would cheapen education
by making it free.   Tell me,' says I, ' which is of the
most value to mankind, literature or horse racing? '

   " ' Why — er —, playing the po — I mean, of
course, the poets and the great writers have got the
call, of course,' says Bill.

"'Exactly,' says I. 'Then why do the master minds of finance and philanthropy,' says I, 'charge us \$2 to get into a race-track and let us into a library

"'*I'm a plain citizen; and I need the job.*'"

free? Is that distilling into the masses,' says I, 'a correct estimate of the relative value of the two means of self-culture and disorder?'

"'You are arguing outside of my faculties of

sense and rhetoric,' says Bill. 'What I wanted you to do is to go to Washington and dig out this appointment for me. I haven't no ideas of cultivation and intrigue. I'm a plain citizen and I need the job. I've killed seven men,' says Bill; 'I've got nine children; I've been a good Republican ever since the first of May; I can't read nor write, and I see no reason why I ain't illegible for the office. And I think your partner, Mr. Tucker,' goes on Bill, 'is also a man of sufficient ingratiation and connected system of mental delinquency to assist you in securing the appointment. I will give you preliminary,' says Bill, '$1,000 for drinks, bribes and carfare in Washington. If you land the job I will pay you $1,000 more, cash down, and guarantee you impunity in boot-legging whiskey for twelve months. Are you patriotic to the West enough to help me put this thing through the Whitewashed Wigwam of the Great Father of the most eastern flag station of the Pennsylvania Railroad?' says Bill.

"Well, I talked to Andy about it, and he liked the idea immense. Andy was a man of an involved nature. He was never content to plod along, as I was, selling to the peasantry some little tool like a combination steak beater, shoe horn, marcel waver,

monkey wrench, nail file, potato masher and Multum
in Parvo tuning fork. Andy had the artistic temper,
which is not to be judged as a preacher's or a moral
man's is by purely commercial deflections. So we
accepted Bill's offer, and strikes out for Washington.

"Says I to Andy, when we get located at a hotel
on South Dakota Avenue, G. S. S. W. ' Now Andy,
for the first time in our lives we've got to do a real
dishonest act. Lobbying is something we've never
been used to; but we've got to scandalize ourselves
for Bill Humble's sake. In a straight and legitimate
business,' says I, ' we could afford to introduce a little
foul play and chicanery, but in a disorderly and hein-
ous piece of malpractice like this it seems to me that
the straightforward and aboveboard way is the best.
I propose,' says I, ' that we hand over $500 of this
money to the chairman of the national campaign committee, get a receipt, lay the receipt on the President's
desk and tell him about Bill. The President is a man
who would appreciate a candidate who went about
getting office that way instead of pulling wires.

"Andy agreed with me, but after we talked the
scheme over with the hotel clerk we give that plan up.
He told us that there was only one way to get an ap-

pointment in Washington, and that was through a lady lobbyist. He gave us the address of one he recommended, a Mrs. Avery, who he said was high up in sociable and diplomatic rings and circles.

" The next morning at 10 o'clock me and Andy called at her hotel, and was shown up to her reception room.

" This Mrs. Avery was a solace and a balm to the eyesight. She had hair the color of the back of a twenty dollar gold certificate, blue eyes and a system of beauty that would make the girl on the cover of a July magazine look like a cook on a Monongahela coal barge.

" She had on a low necked dress covered with silver spangles, and diamond rings and ear bobs. Her arms was bare; and she was using a desk telephone with one hand, and drinking tea with the other.

" ' Well, boys,' says she after a bit, ' what is it?'

" I told her in as few words as possible what we wanted for Bill, and the price we could pay.

" ' Those western appointments,' says she, ' are easy. Le'me see, now,' says she, ' who could put that through for us. No use fooling with Territorial delegates. I guess,' says she, ' that Senator Sniper would be about the man. He's from somewheres in the West. Let's see how he stands on my private

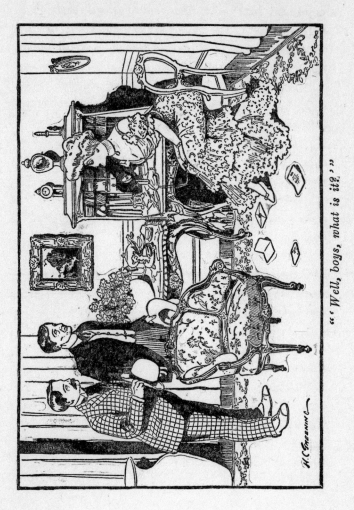

menu card.' She takes some papers out of a pigeon-hole with the letter ' S ' over it.

" ' Yes,' says she, ' he's marked with a star; that means " ready to serve." Now, let's see. " Age 55 ; married twice ; Presbyterian, likes blondes, Tolstoi, poker and stewed terrapin; sentimental at third bottle of wine." Yes,' she goes on, ' I am sure I can have your friend, Mr. Bummer, appointed Minister to Brazil.'

" ' Humble,' says I. ' And United States Marshal was the berth.'

" ' Oh, yes,' says Mrs. Avery. ' I have so many deals of this sort I sometimes get them confused. Give me all the memoranda you have of the case, Mr. Peters, and come back in four days. I think it can be arranged by them.'

" So me and Andy goes back to our hotel and waits. Andy walks up and down and chews the left end of his mustache.

" ' A woman of high intellect and perfect beauty is a rare thing, Jeff,' says he.

" ' As rare,' says I, ' as an omelet made from the eggs of the fabulous bird known as the epidermis,' says I.

" ' A woman like that,' says Andy, ' ought to lead a man to the highest positions of opulence and fame.'

"'I misdoubt,' says I, 'if any woman ever helped a man to secure a job any more than to have his meals ready promptly and spread a report that the other candidate's wife had once been a shoplifter. They are no more adapted for business and politics,' says I, 'than Algernon Charles Swinburne is to be floor manager at one of Chuck Connor's annual balls. I know,' says I to Andy, 'that sometimes a woman seems to step out into the kalsomine light as the charge d'affaires of her man's political job. But how does it come out? Say, they have a neat little berth somewhere as foreign consul of record to Afghanistan or lockkeeper on the Delaware and Raritan Canal. One day this man finds his wife putting on her overshoes and three months supply of bird seed into the canary's cage. "Sioux Falls?" he asks with a kind of hopeful light in his eye. "No, Arthur," says she, "Washington. We're wasted here," says she. "You ought to be Toady Extraordinary to the Court of St. Bridget or Head Porter of the Island of Porto Rico. I'm going to see about it."

"'Then this lady,' I says to Andy, 'moves against the authorities at Washington with her baggage and munitions, consisting of five dozen indiscriminating letters written to her by a member of the Cabinet when she was 15; a letter of introduc-

tion from King Leopold to the Smithsonian Institution, and a pink silk costume with canary colored
spats.

" ' Well, and then what? ' I goes on. ' She has the
letters printed in the evening papers that match her
costume, she lectures at an informal tea given in the
palm room of the B. & O. Depot and then calls on
the President. The ninth Assistant Secretary of
Commerce and Labor, the first aide-de-camp of the
Blue Room and an unidentified colored man are
waiting there to grasp her by the hands — and feet.
They carry her out to S. W. B. street and leave her
on a cellar door. That ends it. The next time we
hear of her she is writing postal cards to the Chinese
Minister asking him to get Arthur a job in a tea
store.'

" ' Then,' says Andy, ' you don't think Mrs.
Avery will land the Marshalship for Bill? '

" ' I do not,' says I. ' I do not wish to be a septic,
but I doubt if she can do as well as you and me
could have done.'

" ' I don't agree with you,' says Andy. ' I'll bet
you she does. I'm proud of having a higher opinion
of the talent and the powers of negotiation of
ladies.'

" We was back at Mrs. Avery's hotel at the time

she appointed. She was looking pretty and fine enough, as far as that went, to make any man let her name every officer in the country. But I hadn't much faith in looks, so I was certainly surprised when she pulls out a document with the great seal of the United States on it, and ' William Henry Humble ' in a fine, big hand on the back.

" You might have had it the next day, boys,' says Mrs. Avery smiling. ' I hadn't the slightest trouble in getting it,' says she. ' I just asked for it, that's all. Now, I'd like to talk to you a while,' she goes on, ' but I'm awfully busy, and I know you'll excuse me. I've got an Ambassadorship, two Consulates and a dozen other minor applications to look after. I can hardly find time to sleep at all. You'll give my compliments to Mr. Humble when you get home, of course.'

" Well, I handed her the $500, which she pitched into her desk drawer without counting. I put Bill's appointment in my pocket and me and Andy made our adieus.

" We started back for the Territory the same day. We wired Bill: ' Job landed; get the tall glasses ready,' and we felt pretty good.

" Andy joshed me all the way about how little I knew about women,

" ' All right,' says I. ' I'll admit that she surprised me.   But it's the first time I ever knew one of 'em to manipulate a piece of business on time without getting it bungled up in some way,' says I.

" Down about the edge of Arkansas I got out Bill's appointment and looked it over, and then I handed it to Andy to read.   Andy read it, but didn't add any remarks to my silence.

" The paper was for Bill, all right, and a genuine document, but it appointed him postmaster of Dade City, Fla.

" Me and Andy got off the train at Little Rock and sent Bill's appointment to him by mail.   Then we struck northeast toward Lake Superior.

" I never saw Bill Humble after that."

THE EXACT SCIENCE OF MATRIMONY

"AS I have told you before," said Jeff Peters, " I never had much confidence in the perfidiousness of woman. As partners or coeducators in the most innocent line of graft they are not trustworthy."

" They deserve the compliment," said I. " I think they are entitled to be called the honest sex."

" Why shouldn't they be? " said Jeff. " They've got the other sex either grafting or working overtime for 'em. They're all right in business until they get their emotions or their hair touched up too much. Then you want to have a flat footed, heavy breathing man with sandy whiskers, five kids and a building and loan mortgage ready as an understudy to take her desk. Now there was that widow lady that me and Andy Tucker engaged to help us in that little matrimonial agency scheme we floated out in Cairo.

" When you've got enough advertising capital — say a roll as big as the little end of a wagon tongue — there's money in matrimonial agencies. We had about $6,000 and we expected to double it in two

months, which is about as long as a scheme like ours
can be carried on without taking out a New Jersey
charter.

"We fixed up an advertisement that read about
like this:

"Charming widow, beautiful, home loving, 32 years, possessing $3,000 cash and owning valuable country property,
would remarry. Would prefer a poor man with affectionate
disposition to one with means, as she realizes that the solid
virtues are oftenest to be found in the humble walks of life.
No objection to elderly man or one of homely appearance if
faithful and true and competent to manage property and
invest money with judgment. Address, with particulars.

LONELY,
Care of Peters & Tucker, agents, Cairo, Ill.

"'So far, so pernicious,' says I, when we had
finished the literary concoction. 'And now,' says I,
'where is the lady?'

"Andy gives me one of his looks of calm irrita-
tion.

"'Jeff,' says he, 'I thought you had lost them
ideas of realism in your art. Why should there be a
lady? When they sell a lot of watered stock on Wall
Street would you expect to find a mermaid in it?
What has a matrimonial ad got to do with a lady?'

"'Now listen,' says I. 'You know my rule, Andy,
that in all my illegitimate inroads against the legal
letter of the law the article sold must be existent,

visible, producible. In that way and by a careful study of city ordinances and train schedules I have kept out of all trouble with the police that a five dollar bill and a cigar could not square. Now, to work this scheme we've got to be able to produce bodily a charming widow or its equivalent with or without the beauty, hereditaments and appurtenances set forth in the catalogue and writ of errors, or hereafter be held by a justice of the peace.'

" 'Well,' says Andy, reconstructing his mind, ' maybe it would be safer in case the post office or the peace commission should try to investigate our agency. But where,' he says, ' could you hope to find a widow who would waste time on a matrimonial scheme that had no matrimony in it? '

" I told Andy that I thought I knew of the exact party. An old friend of mine, Zeke Trotter, who used to draw soda water and teeth in a tent show, had made his wife a widow a year before by drinking some dyspepsia cure of the old doctor's instead of the liniment that he always got boozed up on. I used to stop at their house often, and I thought we could get her to work with us.

" 'Twas only sixty miles to the little town where she lived, so I jumped out on the I. C. and finds her in the same cottage with the same sunflowers and

roosters standing on the washtub. Mrs. Trotter fitted
our ad first rate except, maybe for beauty and age
and property valuation. But she looked feasible and
praiseworthy to the eye, and it was a kindness to
Zeke's memory to give her the job.

"'Is this an honest deal you are putting on, Mr.
Peters,' she asks me when I tell her what we want.

"'Mrs. Trotter,' says I, 'Andy Tucker and me
have computed the calculation that 3,000 men in this
broad and unfair country will endeavor to secure
your fair hand and ostensible money and property
through our advertisement. Out of that number
something like thirty hundred will expect to give you
in exchange, if they should win you, the carcass of
a lazy and mercenary loafer, a failure in life, a swin-
dler and contemptible fortune seeker.

"'Me and Andy,' says I, 'propose to teach these
preyers upon society a lesson. It was with difficulty,'
says I, 'that me and Andy could refrain from form-
ing a corporation under the title of the Great Moral
and Millennial Malevolent Matrimonial Agency.
Does that satisfy you?'

"'It does, Mr. Peters,' says she. 'I might have
known you wouldn't have gone into anything that
wasn't opprobrious. But what will my duties be?
Do I have to reject personally these 3,000 ramscal-

lions you speak of, or can I throw them out in bunches?'

"'Your job, Mrs. Trotter,' says I, 'will be practically a cynosure. You will live at a quiet hotel and will have no work to do. Andy and I will attend to all the correspondence and business end of it.

"'Of course,' says I, 'some of the more ardent and impetuous suitors who can raise the railroad fare may come to Cairo to personally press their suit or whatever fraction of a suit they may be wearing. In that case you will be probably put to the inconvenience of kicking them out face to face. We will pay you $25 per week and hotel expenses.'

"'Give me five minutes,' says Mrs. Trotter, 'to get my powder rag and leave the front door key with a neighbor and you can let my salary begin.'

" So I conveys Mrs. Trotter to Cairo and establishes her in a family hotel far enough away from mine and Andy's quarters to be unsuspicious and available, and I tell Andy.

"'Great,' says Andy. 'And now that your conscience is appeased as to the tangibility and proximity of the bait, and leaving mutton aside, suppose we revenoo a noo fish.'

" So, we began to insert our advertisement in newspapers covering the country far and wide. One ad was all we used. We couldn't have used more without hiring so many clerks and marcelled paraphernalia that the sound of the gum chewing would have disturbed the Postmaster-General.

" We placed $2,000 in a bank to Mrs. Trotter's credit and gave her the book to show in case anybody might question the honesty and good faith of the agency. I knew Mrs. Trotter was square and reliable and it was safe to leave it in her name.

" With that one ad Andy and me put in twelve hours a day answering letters.

" About one hundred a day was what came in. I never knew there was so many large hearted but indigent men in the country who were willing to acquire a charming widow and assume the burden of investing her money.

" Most of them admitted that they ran principally to whiskers and lost jobs and were misunderstood by the world, but all of 'em were sure that they were so chock full of affection and manly qualities that the widow would be making the bargain of her life to get 'em.

" Every applicant got a reply from Peters & Tucker informing him that the widow had been deeply impressed by his straightforward and interesting letter and requesting them to write again;

"*About 100 a day was what came in.*"

stating more particulars; and enclosing photograph
if convenient. Peters & Tucker also informed the
applicant that their fee for handing over the second
letter to their fair client would be $2, enclosed there-
with.

"There you see the simple beauty of the scheme.
About 90 per cent. of them domestic foreign noble-
men raised the price somehow and sent it in. That
was all there was to it. Except that me and Andy
complained an amount about being put to the trouble
of slicing open them envelopes, and taking the money
out.

"Some few clients called in person. We sent 'em
to Mrs. Trotter and she did the rest; except for three
or four who came back to strike us for carfare.
After the letters began to get in from the r. f. d. dis-
tricts Andy and me were taking in about $200 a
day.

"One afternoon when we were busiest and I was
stuffing the two and ones into cigar boxes and Andy
was whistling ' No Wedding Bells for Her ' a small,
slick, man drops in and runs his eye over the walls
like he was on the trail of a lost Gainsborough painting or two. As soon as I saw him I felt a glow of
pride, because we were running our business on the
level.

" ' I see you have quite a large mail to-day,' says the man.

" I reached and got my hat.

" ' Come on,' says I. ' We've been expecting you. I'll show you the goods. How was Teddy when you left Washington? '

" I took him down to the Riverview Hotel and had him shake hands with Mrs. Trotter. Then I showed him her bank book with the $2,000 to her credit.

" ' It seems to be all right,' says the Secret Service.

" ' It is,' says I. ' And if you're not a married man I'll leave you to talk a while with the lady. We won't mention the two dollars.'

" ' Thanks,' says he. ' If I wasn't, I might. Good day, Mrs. Peters.'

" Toward the end of three months we had taken in something over $5,000, and we saw it was time to quit. We had a good many complaints made to us; and Mrs. Trotter seemed to be tired of the job. A good many suitors had been calling to see her, and she didn't seem to like that.

" So we decides to pull out, and I goes down to Mrs. Trotter's hotel to pay her last week's salary and say farewell and get her check for the $2,000.

" When I got there I found her crying like a kid that don't want to go to school.

" ' Now, now,' says I, ' what's it all about? Somebody sassed you or you getting homesick? '

" ' No, Mr. Peters,' says she. ' I'll tell you. You

" ' Mr. Peters, I'm in love.' "

was always a friend of Zeke's, and I don't mind. Mr.
Peters, I'm in love. I just love a man so hard I can't
bear not to get him. He's just the ideal I've always
had in mind.'

" ' Then take him,' says I. ' That is, if it's a mutual case. Does he return the sentiment according to the specifications and painfulness you have described? '

" ' He does,' says she. ' But he's one of the gentlemen that's been coming to see me about the advertisement and he won't marry me unless I give him the $2,000. His name is William Wilkinson.' And then she goes off again in the agitations and hysterics of romance.

" ' Mrs. Trotter,' says I, ' there's no man more sympathizing with a woman's affections than I am. Besides, you was once the life partner of one of my best friends. If it was left to me I'd say take this $2,000 and the man of your choice and be happy.

" ' We could afford to do that, because we have cleaned up over $5,000 from these suckers that wanted to marry you. But,' says I, ' Andy Tucker is to be consulted.

" ' He is a good man, but keen in business. He is my equal partner financially. I will talk to Andy,' says I, ' and see what can be done.'

" I goes back to our hotel and lays the case before Andy.

" ' I was expecting something like this all the time,' says Andy. ' You can't trust a woman to stick by you in any scheme that involves her emotions and preferences.'

" ' It's a sad thing, Andy,' says I, ' to think that we've been the cause of the breaking of a woman's heart.'

" ' It is,' says Andy, ' and I tell you what I'm willing to do, Jeff. You've always been a man of a soft and generous heart and disposition. Perhaps I've been too hard and worldly and suspicious. For once I'll meet you half way. Go to Mrs. Trotter and tell her to draw the $2,000 from the bank and give it to this man she's infatuated with and be happy.'

" I jumps up and shakes Andy's hand for five minutes, and then I goes back to Mrs. Trotter and tells her, and she cries as hard for joy as she did for sorrow.

" Two days afterward me and Andy packed up to go.

" ' Wouldn't you like to go down and meet Mrs. Trotter once before we leave?' I asks him. ' She'd like mightily to know you and express her encomiums and gratitude.'

" ' Why, I guess not," says Andy. ' I guess we'd better hurry and catch that train.'

" I was strapping our capital around me in a memory belt like we always carried it, when Andy pulls a

"'What's this?' says I."

roll of large bills out of his pocket and asks me to put 'em with the rest.

"'What's this?' says I.

"'It Mrs. Trotter's two thousand,' says Andy.

"'How do you come to have it?' I asks.

"'She gave it to me,' says Andy. 'I've been calling on her three evenings a week for more than a month.'

"'Then are you William Wilkinson?' says I,

"'I was,' says Andy."

A MIDSUMMER MASQUERADE

"**SATAN**," said Jeff Peters, " is a hard boss to work for. When other people are having their vacation is when he keeps you the busiest. As old Dr. Watts or St. Paul or some other diagnostician says: ' He always finds somebody for idle hands to do.'

" I remember one summer when me and my partner, Andy Tucker, tried to take a layoff from our professional and business duties; but it seems that our work followed us wherever we went.

" Now, with a preacher it's different. He can throw off his responsibilities and enjoy himself. On the 31st of May he wraps mosquito netting and tin foil around the pulpit, grabs his niblick, breviary and fishing pole and hikes for Lake Como or Atlantic City according to the size of the loudness with which he has been called by his congregation. 'And, sir, for three months he don't have to think about business except to hunt around in Deuteronomy and Proverbs and Timothy to find texts to cover and exculpate such little midsummer penances as dropping a couple of looey door on rouge or teaching a Presbyterian widow to swim.

"But I was going to tell you about mine and Andy's summer vacation that wasn't one.

"We was tired of finance and all the branches of unsanctified ingenuity. Even Andy, whose brain rarely ever stopped working, began to make noises like a tennis cabinet.

"'Heigh ho!' says Andy. 'I'm tired. I've got that steam up the yacht Corsair and ho for the Riviera! feeling. I want to loaf and indict my soul, as Walt Whittier says. I want to play pinochle with Merry del Val or give a knouting to the tenants on my Tarrytown estates or do a monologue at a Chautauqua picnic in kilts or something summery and outside the line of routine sand-bagging.'

"'Patience,' says I. 'You'll have to climb higher in the profession before you can taste the laurels that crown the footprints of the great captains of industry. Now, what I'd like, Andy,' says I, 'would be a summer sojourn in a mountain village far from scenes of larceny, labor and overcapitalization. I'm tired, too, and a month or so of sinlessness ought to leave us in good shape to begin again to take away the white man's burdens in the fall.'

"Andy fell in with the rest cure idea at once, so we

struck the general passenger agents of all the railroads for summer resort literature, and took a week to
study out where we should go. I reckon the first passenger agent in the world was that man Genesis. But
there wasn't much competition in his day, and when
he said: ' The Lord made the earth in six days, and
all very good,' he hadn't any idea to what extent the
press agents of the summer hotels would plagiarize
from him later on.

" When we finished the booklets we perceived, easy,
that the United States from Passadumkeg, Maine, to
El Paso, and from Skagway to Key West was a paradise of glorious mountain peaks, crystal lakes, new
laid eggs, golf, girls, garages, cooling breezes, straw
rides, open plumbing and tennis; and all within two
hours' ride.

" So me and Andy dumps the books out the back
window and packs our trunk and takes the 6 o'clock
Tortoise Flyer for Crow Knob, a kind of a dernier
resort in the mountains on the line of Tennessee and
North Carolina.

" We was directed to a kind of private hotel called
Woodchuck Inn, and thither me and Andy bent and
almost broke our footsteps over the rocks and stumps.
The Inn set back from the road in a big grove of
trees, and it looked fine with its broad porches and a

"Dumps the books out of the back window."

lot of women in white dresses rocking in the shade. The rest of Crow Knob was a post office and some scenery set at an angle of forty-five degrees and a welkin.

"Well, sir, when we got to the gate who do you suppose comes down the walk to greet us? Old Smoke-'em-out Smithers, who used to be the best open air painless dentist and electric liver pad faker in the Southwest.

"Old Smoke-'em-out is dressed clerico-rural, and has the mingled air of a landlord and a claim jumper. Which aspect he corroborates by telling us that he is the host and perpetrator of Woodchuck Inn. I introduces Andy, and we talk about a few volatile topics, such as will go around at meetings of boards of directors and old associates like us three were. Old Smoke-'em-out leads us into a kind of summer house in the yard near the gate and took up the harp of life and smote on all the chords with his mighty right.

" ' Gents,' says he, ' I'm glad to see you. Maybe you can help me out of a scrape. I'm getting a bit old for street work, so I leased this dogdays emporium so the good things would come to me. Two weeks before the season opened I gets a letter signed Lieut. Peary and one from the Duke of Marlborough, each wanting to engage board for part of the summer.

" ' Well, sir, you gents know what a big thing for an obscure hustlery it would be to have for guests two gentlemen whose names are famous from long association with icebergs and the Coburgs. So I prints a lot of handbills announcing that Woodchuck Inn would shelter these distinguished boarders during the summer, except in places where it leaked, and I sends 'em out to towns around as far as Knoxville and Charlotte and Fish Dam and Bowling Green.

" ' And now look up there on the porch, gents,' says Smoke-'em-out, ' at them disconsolate specimens of their fair sex waiting for the arrival of the Duke and the Lieutenant. The house is packed from rafters to cellar with hero worshippers.

" ' There's four normal school teachers and two abnormal; there's three high school graduates between 37 and 42; there's two literary old maids and one that can write; there's a couple of society women and a lady from Haw River. Two elocutionists are bunking in the corn crib, and I've put cots in the hay loft for the cook and the society editress of the Chattanooga *Opera Glass*. You see how names draw, gents.'

" ' Well,' says I, ' how is it that you seem to be biting your thumbs at good luck? You didn't use to be that way.'

" ' I ain't through,' says Smoke-'em-out. ' Yesterday was the day for the advent of the auspicious personages. I goes down to the depot to welcome 'em. Two apparently animate substances gets off the train, both carrying bags full of croquet mallets and these magic lanterns with pushbuttons.

" ' I compares these integers with the original signatures to the letters — and, well, gents, I reckon the mistake was due to my poor eyesight. Instead of being the Lieutenant, the daisy chain and wild verbena explorer was none other than Levi T. Peevy, a soda water clerk from Asheville. And the Duke of Marlborough turned out to be Theo. Drake of Murfreesborough, a bookkeeper in a grocery. What did I do? I kicked 'em both back on the train and watched 'em depart for the lowlands, the low.

" ' Now you see the fix I'm in, gents,' goes on Smoke-'em-out Smithers. ' I told the ladies that the notorious visitors had been detained on the road by some unavoidable circumstances that made a noise like an ice jam and an heiress, but they would arrive a day or two later. When they find out that they've been deceived,' says Smoke-'em-out, ' every yard of cross barred muslin and natural waved switch in the house will pack up and leave. It's a hard deal,' says old Smoke-'em-out.

Instead of the Lieut. and the Duke.

" ' Friend,' says Andy, touching the old man on the æsophagus, ' why this jeremiad when the polar regions and the portals of Blenheim are conspiring to hand you prosperity on a hall-marked silver salver. We have arrived.'

" A light breaks out on Smoke-'em-out's face.

" ' Can you do it, gents? ' he asks. ' Could ye do it? Could ye play the polar man and the little duke for the nice ladies? Will ye do it? '

" I see that Andy is superimposed with his old hankering for the oral and polyglot system of buncoing. That man had a vocabulary of about 10,000 words and synonyms, which arrayed themselves into contraband sophistries and parables when they came out.

" ' Listen,' says Andy to old Smoke-'em-out. ' Can we do it? You behold before you, Mr. Smithers, two of the finest equipped men on earth for inveigling the proletariat, whether by word of mouth, sleight-of-hand or swiftness of foot. Dukes come and go, explorers go and get lost, but me and Jeff Peters,' says Andy, ' go after the come-ons forever. If you say so, we're the two illustrious guests you were expecting. And you'll find,' says Andy, ' that we'll give you the true local color of the title rôles from the aurora borealis to the ducal portcullis.'

"' Can we do it, gents?' he asks."

" Old Smoke-'em-out is delighted. He takes me and Andy up to the inn by an arm apiece, telling us on the way that the finest fruits of the can and luxuries of the fast freights should be ours without price as long as we would stay.

" On the porch Smoke-'em-out says: ' Ladies, I have the honor to introduce His Gracefulness the Duke of Marlborough and the famous inventor of the North Pole, Lieut. Peary.'

" The skirts all flutter and the rocking chairs squeak as me and Andy bows and then goes on in with old Smoke-'em-out to register. And then we washed up and turned our cuffs, and the landlord took us to the rooms he'd been saving for us and got out a demijohn of North Carolina real mountain dew.

" I expected trouble when Andy began to drink. He has the artistic metempsychosis which is half drunk when sober and looks down on airships when stimulated.

" After lingering with the demijohn me and Andy goes out on the porch, where the ladies are to begin to earn our keep. We sit in two special chairs and then the schoolma'ams and literaterrers bunched their rockers close around us.

" One lady says to me: ' How did that last venture of yours turn out, sir? '

" Now, I'd clean forgot to have an understanding with Andy which I was to be, the duke or the lieutenant. And I couldn't tell from her question whether she was referring to Arctic or matrimonial expeditions. So I gave an answer that would cover both cases.

"'Well, ma'am,' says I, ' it was a freeze out — right smart of a freeze out, ma'am.'

"And then the flood gates of Andy's perorations was opened and I knew which one of the renowned ostensible guests I was supposed to be. I wasn't either. Andy was both. And still furthermore it seemed that he was trying to be the mouthpiece of the entire British nobility and of Arctic exploration from Sir John Franklin down. It was the union of corn whiskey and the conscientious fictional form that Mr. W. D. Howletts admires so much.

"'Ladies,' says Andy, smiling semicircularly, 'I am truly glad to visit America. I do not consider the magna charta,' says he, ' or gas balloons or snowshoes in any way a detriment to the beauty and charm of your American women, skyscrapers or the architecture of your icebergs. The next time,' says Andy, 'that I go after the North Pole all the Vanderbilts in Greenland won't be able to turn me out in the cold — I mean make it hot for me.'

"'Tell us about one of your trips, Lieutenant,' says one of the normals.

"'Sure,' says Andy, getting the decision over a hiccup. 'It was in the spring of last year that I sailed the Castle of Blenheim up to latitude 87 degrees Fahrenheit and beat the record. Ladies,' says Andy, 'it was a sad sight to see a Duke allied by a civil and liturgical chattel mortgage to one of your first families lost in a region of semiannual days.' And then he goes on, 'At four bells we sighted Westminster Abbey, but there was not a drop to eat. At noon we threw out five sandbags, and the ship rose fifteen knots higher. At midnight,' continues Andy, 'the restaurants closed. Sitting on a cake of ice we ate seven hot dogs. All around us was snow and ice. Six times a night the boatswain rose up and tore a leaf off the calendar so we could keep time with the barometer. At 12,' says Andy, with a lot of anguish in his face, 'three huge polar bears sprang down the hatchway, into the cabin. And then —'

"'What then, Lieutenant?' says a schoolma'am, excitedly.

" Andy gives a loud sob.

" ' The Duchess shook me,' he cries out, and slides out of the chair and weeps on the porch.

" Well, of course, that fixed the scheme. The women boarders all left the next morning. The landlord wouldn't speak to us for two days, but when he found we had money to pay our way he loosened up.

" So me and Andy had a quiet, restful summer after all, coming away from Crow Knob with $1,100, that we enticed out of old Smoke-'em-out playing seven up."

SHEARING THE WOLF

JEFF PETERS was always eloquent when the ethics of his profession was under discussion.

"The only times," said he, "that me and Andy Tucker ever had any hiatuses in our cordial intents was when we differed on the moral aspects of grafting. Andy had his standards and I had mine. I didn't approve of all of Andy's schemes for levying contributions from the public, and he thought I allowed my conscience to interfere too often for the financial good of the firm. We had high arguments sometimes. Once one word led on to another till he said I reminded him of Rockefeller.

"'I know how you mean that, Andy,' says I, 'but we have been friends too long for me to take offense, at a taunt that you will regret when you cool off. I have yet,' says I, 'to shake hands with a subpœna server.'

"One summer me and Andy decided to rest up a spell in a fine little town in the mountains of Kentucky called Grassdale. We was supposed to be horse drovers, and good decent citizens besides, taking a summer vacation. The Grassdale people liked us, and me and Andy declared a secession of hostilities, never so much as floating the fly leaf of a rubber concession prospectus or flashing a Brazilian diamond while we was there.

" One day the leading hardware merchant of Grassdale drops around to the hotel where me and Andy stopped, and smokes with us, sociable, on the side porch. We knew him pretty well from pitching quoits in the afternoons in the court house yard. He was a loud, red man, breathing hard, but fat and respectable beyond all reason.

" After we talk on all the notorious themes of the day, this Murkison — for such was his entitlements — takes a letter out of his coat pocket in a careful, careless way and hands it to us to read.

" ' Now, what do you think of that? ' says he, laughing — ' a letter like that to ME! '

" Me and Andy sees at a glance what it is; but we pretend to read it through. It was one of them old time typewritten green goods letters explaining how for $1,000 you could get $5,000 in bills that an expert couldn't tell from the genuine; and going on to tell how they were made from plates stolen by an employee of the Treasury at Washington.

"*Pitching quoits in the afternoon in the court house yard.*"

" Think of 'em sending a letter like that to ME!' says Murkison again.

" ' Lot's of good men get 'em,' says Andy. ' If you don't answer the first letter they let you drop. If you answer it they write again asking you to come on with your money and do business.'

" ' But think of 'em writing to ME!' says Murkison.

" A few days later he drops around again.

" ' Boys,' says he, ' I know you are all right or I wouldn't confide in you. I wrote to them rascals again just for fun. They answered and told me to come on to Chicago. They said telegraph to J. Smith when I would start. When I get there I'm to wait on a certain street corner till a man in a gray suit comes along and drops a newspaper in front of me. Then I am to ask him how the water is, and he knows it's me and I know it's him.'

" ' Ah, yes,' says Andy, gaping, ' it's the same old game. I've often read about it in the papers. Then he conducts you to the private abattoir in the hotel, where Mr. Jones is already waiting. They show you brand new real money and sell you all you want at five for one. You see 'em put it in a satchel for you and know it's there. Of course it's brown paper when you come to look at it afterward.'

"*Think of 'em sending a letter like that to ME!*"

"'Oh, they couldn't switch it on me,' says Murkison. 'I haven't built up the best paying business in Grassdale without having witticisms about me. You say it's real money they show you, Mr. Tucker?'

"'I've always—I see by the papers that it always is,' says Andy.

"'Boys,' says Murkison, 'I've got it in my mind that them fellows can't fool me. I think I'll put a couple of thousand in my jeans and go up there and put it all over 'em. If Bill Murkison gets his eyes once on them bills they show him he'll never take 'em off of 'em. They offer $5 for $1, and they'll have to stick to the bargain if I tackle 'em. That's the kind of trader Bill Murkison is. Yes, I jist believe I'll drop up Chicago way and take a 5 to 1 shot on J. Smith. I guess the water'll be fine enough.'

"Me and Andy tries to get this financial misquotation out of Murkison's head, but we might as well have tried to keep the man who rolls peanuts with a toothpick from betting on Bryan's election. No, sir; he was going to perform a public duty by catching these green goods swindlers at their own game. Maybe it would teach 'em a lesson.

"After Murkison left us me and Andy sat a while prepondering over our silent meditations and heresies of reason. In our idle hours we always improved our

"Of course, it's brown paper."

higher selves by ratiocination and mental thought.

" ' Jeff,' says Andy after a long time, ' quite unseldom I have seen fit to impugn your molars when you have been chewing the rag with me about your conscientious way of doing business. I may have been often wrong. But here is a case where I think we can agree. I feel that it would be wrong for us to allow Mr. Murkison to go alone to meet those Chicago green goods men. There is but one way it can end. Don't you think we would both feel better if we was to intervene in some way and prevent the doing of this deed? '

" I got up and shook Andy Tucker's hand hard and long.

" ' Andy,' says I, ' I may have had one or two hard thoughts about the heartlessness of your corporation, but I retract 'em now. You have a kind nucleus at the interior of your exterior after all. It does you credit. I was just thinking the same thing that you have expressed. It would not be honorable or praiseworthy,' says I, ' for us to let Murkison go on with this project he has taken up. If he is determined to go let us go with him and prevent this swindle from coming off.'

" Andy agreed with me; and I was glad to see that

he was in earnest about breaking up this green goods scheme.

"'I don't call myself a religious man,' says I, 'or a fanatic in moral bigotry, but I can't stand still and see a man who has built up a business by his own efforts and brains and risk be robbed by an unscrupulous trickster who is a menace to the public good.'

"'Right, Jeff,' says Andy. 'We'll stick right along with Murkison if he insists on going and block this funny business. I'd hate to see any money dropped in it as bad as you would.'

"Well, we went to see Murkison.

"'No, boys,' says he. 'I can't consent to let the song of this Chicago siren waft by me on the summer breeze. I'll fry some fat out of this ignis fatuus or burn a hole in the skillet. But I'd be plumb diverted to death to have you all go along with me. Maybe you could help some when it comes to cashing in the ticket to that 5 to 1 shot. Yes, I'd really take it as a pastime and regalement if you boys would go along too.'

"Murkison gives it out in Grassdale that he is going for a few days with Mr. Peters and Mr. Tucker to look over some iron ore property in West Virginia. He wires J. Smith that he will set foot in the spider web on a given date; and the three of us lights out for Chicago.

"On the way Murkison amuses himself with premonitions and advance pleasant recollections.

"'In a gray suit,' says he, 'on the southwest corner of Wabash avenue and Lake street. He drops the paper, and I ask how the water is. Oh, my, my, my!' And then he laughs all over for five minutes.

"Sometimes Murkison was serious and tried to talk himself out of his cogitations, whatever they was.

"'Boys,' says he, 'I wouldn't have this to get out in Grassdale for ten times a thousand dollars. It would ruin me there. But I know you all are all right. I think it's the duty of every citizen,' says he, 'to try to do up these robbers that prey upon the public. I'll show 'em whether the water's fine. Five dollars for one — that's what J. Smith offers, and he'll have to keep his contract if he does business with Bill Murkison.'

"We got into Chicago about 7 P. M. Murkison was to meet the gray man at half past 9. We had dinner at a hotel and then went up to Murkison's room to wait for the time to come.

"'Now, boys,' says Murkison, 'let's get our gumption together and inoculate a plan for defeating the enemy. Suppose while I'm exchanging airy bandage with the gray capper you gents come along, by accident, you know, and holler: "Hello, Murk!" and shake hands with symptoms of surprise and familiarity. Then I take the capper aside and tell him you all are Jenkins and Brown of Grassdale, groceries and feed, good men and maybe willing to take a chance while away from home.'

" " " Bring 'em along," he'll say, of course, " if they care to invest." Now, how does that scheme strike you? '

" ' What do you say, Jeff? ' says Andy, looking at me.

" ' Why, I'll tell you what I say,' says I. ' I say let's settle this thing right here now. I don't see any use of wasting any more time.' I took a nickel plated .38 out of my pocket and clicked the cylinder around a few times.

" ' You undevout, sinful, insidious hog,' says I to Murkison, ' get out that two thousand and lay it on the table. Obey with velocity,' says I, ' for otherwise alternatives are impending. I am preferably a man of mildness, but now and then I find myself in the middle of extremities. Such men as you,' I went on after he had laid the money out, ' is what keeps the jails and court houses going. You come up here to rob these men of their money. Does it excuse you? ' I asks, ' that they were trying to skin you? No, sir; you was going to rob Peter to stand off Paul. You are ten times worse,' says I, ' than that green goods man. You go to church at home and pretend to be a decent citizen, but you'll come to Chicago and commit larceny from men that have built up a sound and profitable business by dealing with such contemptible scoundrels as you have tried to be to-day. How do you know,' says I, ' that that green goods man hasn't a large family dependent upon his extortions? It's you supposedly respectable citizens who are always on the lookout to get something for nothing,' says I, ' that support the lotteries and wild-cat mines and stock exchanges and wire tappers of this country. If it wasn't for you they'd go out of business. The green goods man you was going to rob,' says I, ' studied maybe for years to learn his trade. Every turn he makes he risks his money and liberty and maybe his life. You come up here all sanctified and vanoplied with respectability and a pleasing post office address to swindle him. If he gets the money you can squeal to the police. If you get it he hocks the gray suit to buy supper and says nothing. Mr. Tucker and me sized you up,' says I, ' and came along to see that you got what you deserved. Hand over the money,' says I, ' you grass fed hypocrite.'

"I put the two thousand, which was all in $20 bills, in my inside pocket.

"'Now get out your watch,' says I to Murkison. 'No, I don't want it,' says I. 'Lay it on the table and you sit in that chair till it ticks off an hour. Then you can go. If you make any noise or leave any sooner we'll handbill you all over Grassdale. I guess your high position there is worth more than $2,000 to you.'

"Then me and Andy left.

"On the train Andy was a long time silent. Then he says: 'Jeff, do you mind my asking you a question?'

"'Two,' says I, 'or forty.'

"'Was that the idea you had,' says he, 'when we started out with Murkison?'

"'Why, certainly,' says I. 'What else could it have been? Wasn't it yours, too?'

"In about half an hour Andy spoke again. I think there are times when Andy don't exactly understand my system of ethics and moral hygiene.

"'Jeff,' says he, 'some time when you have the leisure I wish you'd draw off a diagram and footnotes of that conscience of yours. I'd like to have it to refer to occasionally.'"

INNOCENTS OF BROADWAY

"I HOPE some day to retire from business," said Jeff Peters; " and when I do I don't want anybody to be able to say that I ever got a dollar of any man's money without giving him a quid pro rata for it. I've always managed to leave a customer some little gewgaw to paste in his scrapbook or stick between his Seth Thomas clock and the wall after we are through trading.

" There was one time I came near having to break this rule of mine and do a profligate and illaudable action, but I was saved from it by the laws and statutes of our great and profitable country.

" One summer me and Andy Tucker, my partner, went to New York to lay in our annual assortment of clothes and gents' furnishings. We was always pompous and regardless dressers, finding that looks went further than anything else in our business, except maybe our knowledge of railroad schedules and an autograph photo of the President that Loeb sent us, probably by mistake. Andy wrote a nature letter once and sent it in about animals that he had seen caught in a trap lots of times. Loeb must have read it ' triplets,' instead of ' trap lots,' and sent the photo. Anyhow, it was useful to us to show people as a guarantee of good faith.

" Me and Andy never cared much to do business in New York. It was too much like pothunting. Catching suckers in that town, is like dynamiting a Texas lake for brass. All you have to do anywhere between the North and East rivers is to stand in the street with an open bag marked, ' Drop packages of money here. No checks or loose bills taken.' You have a cop handy to club pikers who try to chip in post office orders and Canadian money, and that's all there is to New York for a hunter who loves his profession. So me and Andy used to just nature fake the town. We'd get out our spyglasses and watch the woodcocks along the Broadway swamps putting plaster casts on their broken legs, and then we'd sneak away without firing a shot.

" One day in the papier mâché palm room of a chloral hydrate and hops agency in a side street about eight inches off Broadway me and Andy had thrust upon us the acquaintance of a New Yorker. We had beer together until we discovered that each of us knew a man named Hellsmith, traveling for a stove factory in Duluth. This caused us to remark that the world was a very small place, and then this New Yorker busts his string and takes off his tin foil and excelsior packing and starts in giving us his Ellen Terris, beginning with the time he used to sell shoelaces to the Indians on the spot where Tammany Hall now stands.

"This New Yorker had made his money keeping a cigar store in Beekman street, and he hadn't been above Fourteenth street in ten years. Moreover, he had whiskers, and the time has gone by when a true sport will do anything to a man with whiskers. No grafter except a boy who is soliciting subscribers to an illustrated weekly to win the prize air rifle, or a widow, would have the heart to tamper with the man behind with the razor. He was a typical city Reub — I'd bet the man hadn't been out of sight of a skyscraper in twenty-five years.

"Well, presently this metropolitan backwoodsman pulls out a roll of bills with an old blue sleeve elastic fitting tight around it and opens it up.

"'There's $5,000, Mr. Peters,' says he, shoving it over the table to me, 'saved during my fifteen years of business. Put that in your pocket and keep it for me, Mr. Peters. I'm glad to meet you gentlemen from the West, and I may take a drop too much. I want you to take care of my money for me. Now, let's have another beer.'

"'You'd better keep this yourself,' says I. 'We

"*I want you to take care of my money for me.*"

are strangers to you, and you can't trust everybody you meet. Put your roll back in your pocket,' says I. 'And you'd better run along home before some farm-hand from the Kaw River bottoms strolls in here and sells you a copper mine.'

" ' Oh, I don't know,' says Whiskers. ' I guess Little Old New York can take care of herself. I guess I know a man that's on the square when I see him. I've always found the Western people all right. I ask you as a favor, Mr. Peters,' says he, ' to keep that roll in your pocket for me. I know a gentleman when I see him. And now let's have some more beer.'

" In about ten minutes this fall of manna leans back in his chair and snores. Andy looks at me and says: ' I reckon I'd better stay with him for five minutes or so, in case the waiter comes in.'

" I went out the side door and walked half a block up the street. And then I came back and sat down at the table.

" ' Andy,' says I, ' I can't do it. It's too much like swearing off taxes. I can't go off with this man's money without doing something to earn it like taking advantage of the Bankrupt act or leaving a bottle of eczema lotion in his pocket to make it look more like a square deal.'

" ' Well,' says Andy, ' it does seem kind of hard on one's professional pride to lope off with a bearded pard's competency, especially after he has nominated

you custodian of his bundle in the sappy insouciance
of his urban indiscrimination. Suppose we wake him
up and see if we can formulate some commercial
sophistry by which he will be enabled to give us both
his money and a good excuse.'

"We wakes up Whiskers. He stretches himself
and yawns out the hypothesis that he must have
dropped off for a minute. And then he says he
wouldn't mind sitting in at a little gentleman's game
of poker. He used to play some when he attended
high school in Brooklyn; and as he was out for a good
time, why — and so forth.

"Andy brightens up a little at that, for it looks
like it might be a solution to our financial troubles.
So we all three go to our hotel further down Broadway and have the cards and chips brought up to
Andy's room. I tried once more to make this Babe
in the Horticultural Gardens take his five thousand.
But no.

"' Keep that little roll for me, Mr. Peters,' says he,
' and oblige. I'll ask you fer it when I want it. I
guess I know when I'm among friends. A man that's
done business on Beekman street for twenty years,
right in the heart of the wisest little old village on
earth, ought to know what he's about. I guess I
can tell a gentleman from a con man or a flimflammer

when I meet him.   I've got some odd change in my clothes — enough to start the game with, I guess.

"He goes through his pockets and rains $20 gold certificates on the table till it looked like a $10,000 'Autumn Day in a Lemon Grove' picture by Turner in the salons.   Andy almost smiled.

"The first round that was dealt, this boulevardier slaps down his hand, claims low and jack and big casino and rakes in the pot.

"Andy always took a pride in his poker playing. He got up from the table and looked sadly out of the window at the street cars.

"'Well, gentlemen,' says the cigar man, 'I don't blame you for not wanting to play.   I've forgotten the fine points of the game, I guess, it's been so long since I indulged.   Now, how long are you gentlemen going to be in the city?'

"I told him about a week longer.   He says that'll suit him fine.   His cousin is coming over from Brooklyn that evening and they are going to see the sights of New York.   His cousin, he says, is in the artificial limb and lead casket business, and hasn't crossed the bridge in eight years.   They expect to have the time of their lives, and he winds up by asking me to keep his roll of money for him till next day.   I tried to make him take it, but it only insulted him to mention it.

" ' I'll use what I've got in loose change,' says he.
' You keep the rest for me. I'll drop in on you and
Mr. Tucker to-morrow afternoon about 6 or 7,' says
he, ' and we'll have dinner together. Be good.'

" After Whiskers had gone Andy looked at me
curious and doubtful.

" ' Well, Jeff,' says he, ' it looks like the ravens are
trying to feed us two Elijahs so hard that if we
turned 'em down again we ought to have the Audu-
bon Society after us. It won't do to put the crown
aside too often. I know this is something like pater-
nalism, but don't you think Opportunity has skinned
its knuckles about enough knocking at our door? '

" I put my feet on the table and my hands in my
pockets, which is an attitude unfavorable to frivolous
thoughts.

" ' Andy,' says I, ' this man with the hirsute whiskers has got us in a predicament. We can't move
hand or foot with his money. You and me have
got a gentleman's agreement with Fortune that we
can't break. We've done business in the West where
it's more of a fair game. Out there the people we
skin are trying to skin us, even the farmers and the
remittance men that the magazines send out to write
up Goldfields. But there's little sport in New York
city for rod, reel or gun. They hunt here with either

one of two things — a slungshot or a letter of introduction. The town has been stocked so full of carp that the game fish are all gone. If you spread a net here, do you catch legitimate suckers in it, such as the Lord intended to be caught — fresh guys who know it all, sports with a little coin and the nerve to play another man's game, street crowds out for the fun of dropping a dollar or two and village smarties who know just where the little pea is? No, sir,' says I. 'What the grafters live on here is widows and orphans, and foreigners who save up a bag of money and hand it out over the first counter they see with an iron railing to it, and factory girls and little shop-keepers that never leave the block they do business on. That's what they call suckers here. They're nothing but canned sardines, and all the bait you need to catch 'em is a pocketknife and a soda cracker.

"'Now, this cigar man,' I went on, 'is one of the types. He's lived twenty years on one street without learning as much as you would in getting a once-over shave from a lockjawed barber in a Kansas crossroads town. But he's a New Yorker, and he'll brag about that all the time when he isn't picking up live wires or getting in front of street cars or paying out money to wire-tappers or standing under a safe that's being hoisted into a sky-scraper. When a New

Yorker does loosen up,' says I, ' it's like the spring decomposition of the ice jam in the Allegheny River. He'll swamp you with cracked ice and backwater if you don't get out of the way.

"'It's mighty lucky for us, Andy,' says I, ' that this cigar exponent with the parsley dressing saw fit to bedeck us with his childlike trust and altruism. For,' says I, ' this money of his is an eyesore to my sense of rectitude and ethics. We can't take it, Andy; you know we can't,' says I, ' for we haven't a shadow of a title to it — not a shadow. If there was the least bit of a way we could put in a claim to it I'd be willing to see him start in for another twenty years and make another $5,000 for himself, but we haven't sold him anything, we haven't been embroiled in a trade or anything commercial. He approached us friendly,' says I, ' and with blind and beautiful idiocy laid the stuff in our hands. We'll have to give it back to him when he wants it.'

"'Your arguments,' says Andy, ' are past criticism or comprehension. No, we can't walk off with the money — as things now stand. I admire your conscious way of doing business, Jeff,' says Andy, ' and I wouldn't propose anything that wasn't square in line with your theories of morality and initiative.

"'But I'll be away to-night and most of to-morrow

" We can't take it, Andy."

'Jeff,' says Andy. 'I've got some business affairs that I want to attend to. When this free greenbacks party comes in to-morrow afternoon hold him here till I arrive. We've all got an engagement for dinner, you know.'

" Well, sir, about 5 the next afternoon in trips the cigar man, with his eyes half open.

" ' Been having a glorious time, Mr. Peters,' says he. ' Took in all the sights. I tell you New York is the onliest only. Now if you don't mind,' says he, ' I'll lie down on that couch and doze off for about nine minutes before Mr. Tucker comes. I'm not used to being up all night. And to-morrow, if you don't mind, Mr. Peters, I'll take that five thousand. I met a man last night that's got a sure winner at the race-track to-morrow. Excuse me for being so impolite as to go to sleep, Mr. Peters.'

" And so this inhabitant of the second city in the world reposes himself and begins to snore, while I sit there musing over things and wishing I was back in the West, where you could always depend on a customer fighting to keep his money hard enough to let your conscience take it from him.

" At half-past 5 Andy come in and sees the sleeping form.

" ' I've been over to Trenton,' says Andy, pulling

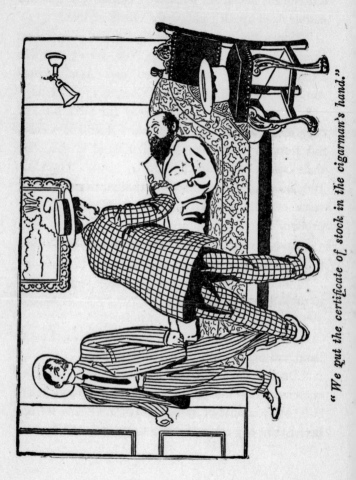

"*We put the certificate of stock in the cigarman's hand.*"

a document out of his pocket. 'I think I've got this matter fixed up all right, Jeff. Look at that.'

"I open the paper and see that it is a corporation charter issued by the State of New Jersey to 'The Peters & Tucker Consolidated and Amalgamated Aerial Franchise Development Company, Limited.'

"'It's to buy up rights of way for airship lines,' explained Andy. 'The Legislature wasn't in session, but I found a man at a postcard stand in the lobby that kept a stock of charters on hand. There are 100,000 shares,' says Andy, 'expected to reach a par value of $1. I had one blank certificate of stock printed.'

"Andy takes out the blank and begins to fill it in with a fountain pen.

"'The whole bunch,' says he, 'goes to our friend in dreamland for $5,000. Did you learn his name?'

"'Make it out to bearer,' says I.

"We put the certificate of stock in the cigar man's hand and went out to pack our suit cases.

"On the ferryboat Andy says to me: 'Is your conscience easy about taking the money now, Jeff?'

"'Why shouldn't it be?' says I. 'Are we any better than any other Holding Corporation?'"

"I NEVER could hold my partner, Andy Tucker, down to legitimate ethics of pure swindling," said Jeff Peters to me one day.

"Andy had too much imagination to be honest. He used to devise schemes of money-getting so fraudulent and high-financial that they wouldn't have been allowed in the bylaws of a railroad rebate system.

"Myself, I never believed in taking any man's dollars unless I gave him something for it — something in the way of rolled gold jewelry, garden seeds, lumbago lotion, stock certificates, stove polish or a crack on the head to show for his money. I guess I must have had New England ancestors away back and inherited some of their stanch and rugged fear of the police.

"But Andy's family tree was in different kind. I don't think he could have traced his descent any further back than a corporation.

"One summer while we was in the middle West, working down the Ohio valley with a line of family

126

albums, headache powders and roach destroyer, Andy takes one of his notions of high and actionable financiering.

" ' Jeff,' says he, ' I've been thinking that we ought to drop these rutabaga fanciers and give our attention to something more nourishing and prolific. If we keep on snapshooting these hinds for their egg money we'll be classed as nature fakers. How about plunging into the fastnesses of the skyscraper country and biting some big bull caribous in the chest? '

" ' Well,' says I, ' you know my idiosyncrasies. I prefer a square, non-illegal style of business such as we are carrying on now. When I take money I want to leave some tangible object in the other fellow's hands for him to gaze at and to distract his attention from my spoor, even if it's only a Komical Kuss Trick Finger Ring for Squirting Perfume in a Friend's Eye. But if you've got a fresh idea, Andy,' says I, ' let's have a look at it. I'm not so wedded to petty graft that I would refuse something better in the way of a subsidy.'

" ' I was thinking,' says Andy, ' of a little hunt without horn, hound or camera among the great herd of the Midas Americanus, commonly known as the Pittsburg millionaires.'

" ' In New York? ' I asks.

"'No, sir,' says Andy, 'in Pittsburg. That's their habitat. They don't like New York. They go there now and then just because it's expected of 'em.'

"'A Pittsburg millionaire in New York is like a fly in a cup of hot coffee — he attracts attention and comment, but he don't enjoy it. New York ridicules him for "blowing" so much money in that town of sneaks and snobs, and sneers. The truth is, he don't spend anything while he is there. I saw a memorandum of expenses for a ten days trip to Bunkum Town made by a Pittsburg man worth $15,000,000 once. Here's the way he set it down:

R. R. fare to and from............................	$21 00
Cab fare to and from hotel........................	2 00
Hotel bill @ $5 per day............................	50 00
Tips	5,750 00
Total	$5,823 00

"'That's the voice of New York,' goes on Andy. 'The town's nothing but a head waiter. If you tip it too much it'll go and stand by the door and make fun of you to the hat check boy. When a Pittsburger wants to spend money and have a good time he stays at home. That's where we'll go to catch him.'

"Well, to make a dense story more condensed, me and Andy cached our paris green and antipyrine powders and albums in a friend's cellar, and took the trail to Pittsburg. Andy didn't have any especial prospectus of chicanery and violence drawn up, but he always had plenty of confidence that his immoral nature would rise to any occasion that presented itself.

" As a concession to my ideas of self-preservation and rectitude he promised that if I should take an active and incriminating part in any little business venture that we might work up there should be something actual and cognizant to the senses of touch, sight, taste or smell to transfer to the victim for the money so my conscience might rest easy. After that I felt better and entered more cheerfully into the foul play.

" ' Andy,' says I, as we strayed through the smoke along the cinderpath they call Smithfield street, ' had you figured out how we are going to get acquainted with these coke kings and pig iron squeezers? Not that I would decry my own worth or system of drawing room deportment, and work with the olive fork and pie knife,' says I, ' but isn't the entree nous into the salons of the stogie smokers going to be harder than you imagined? '

" ' If there's any handicap at all,' says Andy, ' it's our own refinement and inherent culture. Pittsburg millionaires are a fine body of plain, wholehearted, unassuming, democratic men.

" ' They are rough but uncivil in their manners, and though their ways are boisterous and unpolished, under it all they have a great deal of impoliteness and discourtesy. Nearly every one of 'em rose from obscurity,' says Andy, ' and they'll live in it till the town gets to using smoke consumers. If we act simple and unaffected and don't go too far from the saloons and keep making a noise like an import duty on steel rails we won't have any trouble in meeting some of 'em socially.'

" Well Andy and me drifted about town three or four days getting our bearings. We got to knowing several millionaires by sight.

" One used to stop his automobile in front of our hotel and have a quart of champagne brought out to him. When the waiter opened it he'd turn it up to his mouth and drink it out of the bottle. That showed he used to be a glassblower before he made his money.

" One evening Andy failed to come to the hotel for dinner. About 11 o'clock he came into my room.

" ' Landed one, Jeff,' says he. ' Twelve millions. Oil, rolling mills, real estate and natural gas. He's a fine man; no airs about him. Made all his money in the last five years. He's got professors posting him

up now in education — art and literature and haberdashery and such things.

" ' When I saw him he'd just won a bet of $10,000
with a Steel Corporation man that there'd be four
suicides in the Allegheny rolling mills to-day. So
everybody in sight had to walk up and have drinks
on him. He took a fancy to me and asked me to dinner with him. We went to a restaurant in Diamond
alley and sat on stools and had sparkling Moselle and
clam chowder and apple fritters.

" ' Then he wanted to show me his bachelor apartment on Liberty street. He's got ten rooms over a
fish market with privilege of the bath on the next
floor above. He told me it cost him $18,000 to fur-
nish his apartment, and I believe it.

" ' He's got $40,000 worth of pictures in one
room, and $20,000 worth of curios and antiques in
another. His name's Scudder, and he's 45, and taking lessons on the piano and 15,000 barrels of oil a
day out of his wells.

" ' All right,' says I. ' Preliminary canter satis-
factory. But, kay vooly, voo? What good is the
art junk to us? And the oil? '

" ' Now, that man,' says Andy, sitting thought-
fully on the bed, ' ain't what you would call an ordinary scutt. When he was showing me his cabinet of

art curios his face lighted up like the door of a coke oven. He says that if some of his big deals go through he'll make J. P. Morgan's collection of sweatshop tapestry and Augusta, Me., beadwork look like the contents of an ostrich's craw thrown on a screen by a magic lantern.

" ' And then he showed me a little carving,' went on Andy, ' that anybody could see was a wonderful thing. It was something like 2,000 years old, he said. It was a lotus flower with a woman's face in it carved out of a solid piece of ivory.

" Scudder looks it up in a catalogue and describes it. An Egyptian carver named Khafra made two of 'em for King Rameses II. about the year B. C. The other one can't be found. The junkshops and antique bugs have rubbered all Europe for it, but it seems to be out of stock. Scudder paid $2,000 for the one he has.'

" ' Oh, well,' says I, ' this sounds like the purling of a rill to me. I thought we came here to teach the millionaires business, instead of learning art from 'em? '

" ' Be patient,' says Andy, kindly. ' Maybe we will see a rift in the smoke ere long.'

" All the next morning Andy was out. I didn't see him until about noon. He came to the hotel and called me into his room across the hall. He pulled a roundish bundle about as big as a goose egg out of his pocket and unwrapped it. It was an ivory carving just as he had described the millionaire's to me.

"'I went in an old second hand store and pawnshop a while ago,' says Andy, 'and I see this half hidden under a lot of old daggers and truck. The pawnbroker said he'd had it several years and thinks it was soaked by some Arabs or Turks or some foreign dubs that used to live down by the river.

"'I offered him $2 for it, and I must have looked like I wanted it, for he said it would be taking the pumpernickel out of his children's mouths to hold any conversation that did not lead up to a price of $35. I finally got it for $25.

"'Jeff,' goes on Andy, 'this is the exact counterpart of Scudder's carving. It's absolutely a dead ringer for it. He'll pay $2,000 for it as quick as he'd tuck a napkin under his chin. And why shouldn't it be the genuine other one, anyhow, that the old gypsy whittled out?'

"'Why not, indeed?' says I. 'And how shall we go about compelling him to make a voluntary purchase of it?'

"Andy had his plan all ready, and I'll tell you how we carried it out.

" I got a pair of blue spectacles, put on my black frock coat, rumpled my hair up and became Prof. Pickleman. I went to another hotel, registered, and sent a telegram to Scudder to come to see me at once on important art business. The elevator dumped him on me in less than an hour. He was a foggy man with a clarion voice, smelling of Connecticut wrappers and naphtha.

" ' Hello, Profess ! ' he shouts. ' How's your conduct? '

" I rumpled my hair some more and gave him a blue glass stare.

" ' Sir,' says I. ' Are you Cornelius T. Scudder? Of Pittsburg, Pennsylvania? '

" ' I am,' says he. ' Come out and have a drink.'

" ' I have neither the time nor the desire,' says I, ' for such harmful and deleterious amusements. I have come from New York,' says I, ' on a matter of busi — on a matter of art.

" ' I learned there that you are the owner of an Egyptian ivory carving of the time of Rameses II., representing the head of Queen Isis in a lotus flower. There were only two of such carvings made. One has been lost for many years. I recently discovered and purchased the other in a pawn — in an obscure

museum in Vienna. I wish to purchase yours.
Name your price.'

"'Well, the great ice jams, Profess!' says Scudder. 'Have you found the other one? Me sell?
No. I don't guess Cornelius Scudder needs to sell
anything that he wants to keep. Have you got the
carving with you, Profess?'

" I shows it to Scudder. He examines it careful
all over.

"'It's the article,' says he. 'It's a duplicate of
mine, every line and curve of it. Tell you what I'll
do,' he says. 'I won't sell, but I'll buy. Give you
$2,500 for yours.'

"'Since you won't sell, I will,' says I. 'Large
bills, please. I'm a man of few words. I must return to New York to-night. I lecture to-morrow at
the aquarium.'

" Scudder sends a check down and the hotel cashes
it. He goes off with his piece of antiquity and I
hurry back to Andy's hotel, according to arrangement.

"Andy is walking up and down the room looking
at his watch.

"'Well?' he says.

"'Twenty-five hundred,' says I. 'Cash.'

" ' We've got just eleven minutes,' says Andy, ' to catch the B. & O. westbound.   Grab your baggage.'

" ' What's the hurry,' says I.   ' It was a square deal.   And even if it was only an imitation of the original carving it'll take him some time to find it out.   He seemed to be sure it was the genuine article.'

" ' It was,' says Andy.   ' It was his own.   When I was looking at his curios yesterday he stepped out of the room for a moment and I pocketed it.   Now, will you pick up your suit case and hurry? '

" ' Then,' says I, ' why was that story about finding another one in the pawn —"

" ' Oh,' says Andy, ' out of respect for that conscience of yours.   Come on.' "

THE MAN HIGHER UP

ACROSS our two dishes of spaghetti, in a corner of Provenzano's restaurant, Jeff Peters was explaining to me the three kinds of graft.

Every winter Jeff comes to New York to eat spaghetti, to watch the shipping in East River from the depths of his chinchilla overcoat, and to lay in a supply of Chicago-made clothing at one of the Fulton street stores. During the other three seasons he may be found further west — his range is from Spokane to Tampa. In his profession he takes a pride which he supports and defends with a serious and unique philosophy of ethics. His profession is no new one. He is an incorporated, uncapitalized, unlimited asylum for the reception of the restless and unwise dollars of his fellowmen.

In the wilderness of stone in which Jeff seeks his annual lonely holiday he is glad to palaver of his many adventures, as a boy will whistle after sundown in a wood. Wherefore, I mark on my calendar the time of his coming, and open a question of privilege at Provenzano's concerning the little wine-stained table in the corner between the rakish rubber plant and the framed palazzio della something on the wall.

"There are two kinds of grafts," said Jeff, "that ought to be wiped out by law. I mean Wall Street speculation, and burglary."

"Nearly everybody will agree with you as to one of them," said I, with a laugh.

"Well, burglary ought to be wiped out, too," said Jeff; and I wondered whether the laugh had been redundant.

"About three months ago," said Jeff, "it was my privilege to become familiar with a sample of each of the aforesaid branches of illegitimate art. I was *sine qua grata* with a member of the housebreakers' union and one of the John D. Napoleons of finance at the same time."

"Interesting combination," said I, with a yawn. "Did I tell you I bagged a duck and a ground-squirrel at one shot last week over in the Ramapos?" I knew well how to draw Jeff's stories.

"Let me tell you first about these barnacles that clog the wheels of society by poisoning the springs of rectitude with their upas-like eye," said Jeff, with the pure gleam of the muck-raker in his own.

"As I said, three months ago I got into bad com-

pany. There are two times in a man's life when he
does this — when he's dead broke, and when he's
rich.

"Now and then the most legitimate business runs
out of luck. It was out in Arkansas I made the
wrong turn at a cross-road, and drives into this town
of Peavine by mistake. It seems I had already as-
saulted and disfigured Peavine the spring of the year
before. I had sold $600 worth of young fruit trees
there — plums, cherries, peaches and pears. The
Peaviners were keeping an eye on the country road
and hoping I might pass that way again. I drove
down Main street as far as the Crystal Palace drug-
store before I realized I had committed ambush upon
myself and my white horse Bill.

"The Peaviners took me by surprise and Bill by
the bridle and began a conversation that wasn't en-
tirely disassociated with the subject of fruit trees.
A committee of 'em ran some trace-chains through
the armholes of my vest, and escorted me through
their gardens and orchards.

"Their fruit trees hadn't lived up to their labels.
Most of 'em had turned out to be persimmons and
dogwoods, with a grove or two of blackjacks and
poplars. The only one that showed any signs of
bearing anything was a fine young cottonwood that

had put forth a hornet's nest and half of an old corset-cover.

"The Peaviners protracted our fruitless stroll to the edge of town. They took my watch and money on account; and they kept Bill and the wagon as hostages. They said the first time one of them dogwood trees put forth an Amsden's June peach I might come back and get my things. Then they took off the trace-chains and jerked their thumbs in the direction of the Rocky Mountains; and I struck a Lewis and Clark lope for the swollen rivers and impenetrable forests.

"When I regained intellectualness I found myself walking into an unidentified town on the A., T. & S. F. railroad. The Peaviners hadn't left anything in my pockets except a plug of chewing — they wasn't after my life — and that saved it. I bit off a chunk and sits down on a pile of ties by the track to recogitate my sensations of thought and perspicacity.

"And then along comes a fast freight which slows up a little at the town; and off of it drops a black bundle that rolls for twenty yards in a cloud of dust and then gets up and begins to spit soft coal and interjections. I see it is a young man broad across the face, dressed more for Pullmans than freights, and with a cheerful kind of smile in spite of it all that made Phœbe Snow's job look like a chimney-sweep's.

"'Fall off?' says I.

"'Nunk,' says he. 'Got off. Arrived at my destination. What town is this?'

"'Haven't looked it up on the map yet,' says I. 'I got in about five minutes before you did. How does it strike you?'

"'Hard,' says he, twisting one of his arms around. 'I believe that shoulder — no, it's all right.'

"He stoops over to brush the dust off his clothes, when out of his pocket drops a fine, nine-inch burglar's steel jimmy. He picks it up and looks at me sharp, and then grins and holds out his hand.

"'Brother,' says he, 'greetings. Didn't I see you in Southern Missouri last summer selling colored sand at half-a-dollar a teaspoonful to put into lamps to keep the oil from exploding?'

"'Oil,' says I, 'never explodes. It's the gas that forms that explodes.' But I shakes hands with him, anyway.

"'My name's Bill Bassett,' says he to me, 'and if you'll call it professional pride instead of conceit, I'll inform you that you have the pleasure of meeting the best burglar that ever set a gum-shoe on ground drained by the Mississippi River.'

"Well, me and this Bill Bassett sits on the ties and exchanges brags as artists in kindred lines will do. It seems he didn't have a cent, either, and we went into close caucus. He explained why an able burglar sometimes had to travel on freights by telling me that a servant girl had played him false in Little Rock, and he was making a quick get-away.

"'It's part of my business,' says Bill Bassett, 'to play up to the ruffles when I want to make a riffle as Raffles. 'Tis loves that makes the bit go 'round. Show me a house with the swag in it and a pretty parlor-maid, and you might as well call the silver melted down and sold, and me spilling truffles and that Château stuff on the napkin under my chin, while the police are calling it an inside job just because the old lady's nephew teaches a Bible class. I first make an impression on the girl,' says Bill, 'and when she lets me inside I make an impression on the locks. But this one in Little Rock done me,' says he. 'She saw me taking a trolley ride with another girl, and when I came 'round on the night she was to leave the door open for me it was fast. And I had keys made for the doors upstairs. But, no sir. She had sure cut off my locks. She was a Delilah,' says Bill Bassett.

"It seems that Bill tried to break in anyhow with his jimmy, but the girl emitted a succession of bravura noises like the top-riders of a tally-ho, and Bill had to take all the hurdles between there and the depot. As he had no baggage they tried hard to check his departure, but he made a train that was just pulling out.

"'Well,' says Bill Bassett, when we had exchanged memoirs of our dead lives, 'I could eat. This town don't look like it was kept under a Yale lock. Suppose we commit some mild atrocity that will bring in temporary expense money. I don't suppose you've brought along any hair tonic or rolled gold watch-chains, or similar law-defying swindles that you could sell on the plaza to the pikers of the paretic populace, have you?'

"'No,' says I, 'I left an elegant line of Patagonian diamond earrings and rainy-day sunbursts in my valise at Peavine. But they're to stay there till some of them black-gum trees begin to glut the market with yellow clings and Japanese plums. I reckon we can't count on them unless we take Luther Burbank in for a partner.'

"'Very well,' says Bassett, 'we'll do the best we can. Maybe after dark I'll borrow a hairpin from some lady, and open the Farmers and Drovers Marine Bank with it.'

"While we were talking, up pulls a passenger train

to the depot near by. A person in a high hat gets off on the wrong side of the train and comes tripping down the track towards us. He was a little, fat man with a big nose and rat's eyes, but dressed expensive, and carrying a hand-satchel careful, as if it had eggs or railroad bonds in it. He passes by us and keeps on down the track, not appearing to notice the town.

"'Come on,' says Bill Bassett to me, starting after him.

"'Where?' I asks.

"'Lordy!' says Bill, 'had you forgot you was in the desert? Didn't you see Colonel Manna drop down right before your eyes? Don't you hear the rustling of General Raven's wings? I'm surprised at you, Elijah.'

"We overtook the stranger in the edge of some woods, and, as it was after sun-down and in a quiet place, nobody saw us stop him. Bill takes the silk hat off the man's head and brushes it with his sleeve and puts it back.

"'What does this mean, sir?' says the man.

"'When I wore one of these,' says Bill, 'and felt embarrassed, I always done that. Not having one now I had to use yours. I hardly know how to begin, sir, in explaining our business with you, but I guess we'll try your pockets first.'

" Bill Bassett felt in all of them, and looked disgusted.

" ' Not even a watch,' he says. ' Ain't you ashamed of yourself, you whited sculpture? Going about dressed like a head-waiter, and financed like a Count! You haven't even got carfare. What did you do with your transfer? '

" The man speaks up and says he has no assets or valuables of any sort. But Bassett takes his handsatchel and opens it. Out comes some collars and socks and a half a page of a newspaper clipped out. Bill reads the clipping careful, and holds out his hand to the held-up party.

" ' Brother,' says he, ' greetings! Accept the apologies of friends. I am Bill Bassett, the burglar. Mr. Peters, you must make the acquaintance of Mr. Alfred E. Ricks. Shake hands. Mr. Peters,' says Bill, ' stands about halfway between me and you, Mr. Ricks, in the line of havoc and corruption. He always gives something for the money he gets. I'm glad to meet you, Mr. Ricks— you and Mr. Peters. This is the first time I ever attended a full gathering of the National Synod of Sharks — housebreaking, swindling, and financiering all represented. Please examine Mr. Rick's credentials, Mr. Peters.'

" The piece of newspaper that Bill Bassett handed

me had a good picture of this Ricks on it. It was a
Chicago paper, and it had obloquies of Ricks in every
paragraph. By reading it over I harvested the intelligence that said alleged Ricks had laid off all that
portion of the State of Florida that lies under water
into town lots and sold 'em to alleged innocent investors from his magnificently furnished offices in
Chicago. After he had taken in a hundred thousand
or so dollars one of these fussy purchasers that are
always making trouble (I've had 'em actually try gold
watches I've sold 'em with acid) took a cheap excursion down to the land where it is always just before
supper to look at his lot and see if it didn't need a
new paling or two on the fence, and market a few
lemons in time for the Christmas present trade. He
hires a surveyor to find his lot for him. They run
the line out and find the flourishing town of Paradise
Hollow, so advertised, to be about 40 rods and 16
poles S., 27° E. of the middle of Lake Okeechobee.
This man's lot was under thirty-six feet of water,
and, besides, had been preëmpted so long by the alligators and gars that his title looked fishy.

"Naturally, the man goes back to Chicago and
makes it as hot for Alfred E. Ricks as the morning
after a prediction of snow by the weather bureau.
Ricks defied the allegation, but he couldn't deny the

alligators. One morning the papers came out with
a column about it, and Ricks come out by the fire-
escape. It seems the alleged authorities had beat him
to the safe-deposit box where he kept his winnings,
and Ricks has to westward ho! with only feetwear
and a dozen 15½ English pokes in his shopping bag.
He happened to have some mileage left in his book,
and that took him as far as the town in the wilderness where he was spilled out on me and Bill Bassett
as Elijah III. with not a raven in sight for any of us.

"Then this Alfred E. Ricks lets out a squeak that
he is hungry, too, and denies the hypothesis that he
is good for the value, let alone the price, of a meal.
And so, there was the three of us, representing, *if*
we had a mind to draw syllogisms and parabolas,
labor and trade and capital. Now, when trade has no
capital there isn't a dicker to be made. And when
capital has no money there's a stagnation in steak
and onions. That put it up to the man with the
jimmy.

" ' Brother bushrangers,' says Bill Bassett, ' never
yet, in trouble, did I desert a pal. Hard by, in yon
wood, I seem to see unfurnished lodgings. Let us go
there and wait till dark.'

"There was an old, deserted cabin in the grove,
and we three took possession of it. After dark Bill

Bassett tells us to wait, and goes out for half an hour. He comes back with a armful of bread and spareribs and pies.

"'Panhandled 'em at a farmhouse on Washita Avenue,' says he. 'Eat, drink and be leary.'

"The full moon was coming up bright, so we sat on the floor of the cabin and ate in the light of it. And this Bill Bassett begins to brag.

"'Sometimes,' says he, with his mouth full of country produce, 'I lose all patience with you people that think you are higher up in the profession than I am. Now, what could either of you have done in the present emergency to set us on our feet again? Could you do it, Ricksy?'

"'I must confess, Mr. Bassett,' says Ricks, speaking nearly inaudible out of a slice of pie, 'that at this immediate juncture I could not, perhaps, promote an enterprise to relieve the situation. Large operations, such as I direct, naturally require careful preparation in advance. I—'

"'I know, Ricksy,' breaks in Bill Bassett. 'You needn't finish. You need $500 to make the first payment on a blond typewriter, and four roomsful of quartered oak furniture. And you need $500 more for advertising contracts. And you need two weeks' time for the fish to begin to bite. Your line of relief would be about as useful in an emergency as advocating municipal ownership to cure a man suffocated by eighty-cent gas. And your graft ain't much swifter, Brother Peters,' he winds up.

" ' Oh,' says I, ' I haven't seen you turn anything into gold with your wand yet, Mr. Good Fairy. 'Most anybody could rub the magic ring for a little left-over victuals.'

" ' That was only getting the pumpkin ready,' says Bassett, braggy and cheerful. ' The coach and six'll drive up to the door before you know it, Miss Cinderella. Maybe you've got some scheme under your sleeve-holders that will give us a start.'

" ' Son,' says I, ' I'm fifteen years older than you are, and young enough yet to take out an endowment policy. I've been broke before. We can see the lights of that town not half a mile away. I learned under Montague Silver, the greatest street man that ever spoke from a wagon. There are hundreds of men walking those streets this moment with grease spots on their clothes. Give me a gasoline lamp, a dry-goods box, and a two-dollar bar of white castile soap, cut into little —'

" ' Where's your two dollars? ' snickered Bill Bassett into my discourse. There was no use arguing with that burglar.

" 'No,' he goes on; 'you're both babes-in-the-wood. Finance has closed the mahogany desk, and trade has put the shutters up. Both of you look to labor to start the wheels going. All right. You admit it. To-night I'll show you what Bill Bassett can do.'

" Bassett tells me and Ricks not to leave the cabin till he comes back, even if it's daylight, and then he starts off toward town, whistling gay.

" This Alfred E. Ricks pulls off his shoes and his coat, lays a silk handkerchief over his hat, and lays down on the floor.

" 'I think I will endeavor to secure a little slumber,' he squeaks. 'The day has been fatiguing. Good-night, my dear Mr. Peters.'

" 'My regards to Morpheus,' says I. 'I think I'll sit up a while.'

" About two o'clock, as near as I could guess by my watch in Peavine, home comes our laboring man and kicks up Ricks, and calls us to the streak of bright moonlight shining in the cabin door. Then he spreads out five packages of one thousand dollars each on the floor, and begins to cackle over the nest-egg like a hen.

" 'I'll tell you a few things about that town,' says he. 'It's named Rocky Springs, and they're building a Masonic temple, and it looks like the Democratic candidate for mayor is going to get soaked by a Pop, and Judge Tucker's wife, who has been down with pleurisy, is some better. I had a talk on these liliputian thesises before I could get a siphon in the fountain of knowledge that I was after. And there's a bank there called the Lumberman's Fidelity and Plowman's Savings Institution. It closed for business yesterday with $23,000 cash on hand. It will open this morning with $18,000 — all silver — that's the reason I didn't bring more. There you are, trade and capital. Now, will you be bad?'

"'My young friend,' says Alfred E. Ricks, holding up his hands, 'have you robbed this bank? Dear me, dear me!'

"'You couldn't call it that,' says Bassett. '"Robbing" sounds harsh. All I had to do was to find out what street it was on. That town is so quiet that I could stand on the corner and hear the tumblers clicking in that safe lock —" right to 45; left twice to 80; right once to 60; left to 15 "— as plain as the Yale captain giving orders in the football dialect. Now, boys,' says Bassett, 'this is an early rising town. They tell me the citizens are all up and stirring before daylight. I asked what for, and they said because breakfast was ready at that time. And what of merry,

Robin Hood? It must be Yoicks! and away with the tinkers' chorus. I'll stake you. How much do you want? Speak up. Capital.'

" ' My dear young friend,' says this ground squirrel of a Ricks, standing on his hind legs and juggling nuts in his paws, ' I have friends in Denver who would assist me. If I had a hundred dollars I —'

" Bassett unpins a package of the currency and throws five twenties to Ricks.

" ' Trade, how much? ' he says to me.

" ' Put your money up, Labor,' says I. ' I never yet drew upon honest toil for its hard-earned pittance. The dollars I get are surplus ones that are burning the pockets of damfools and greenhorns. When I stand on a street corner and sell a solid gold diamond ring to a yap for $3.00, I make just $2.60. And I know he's going to give it to a girl in return for all the benefits accruing from a $125.00 ring. His profits are $122.00. Which of us is the biggest fakir? '

" ' And when you sell a poor woman a pinch of sand for fifty cents to keep her lamp from exploding,' says Bassett, ' what do you figure her gross earnings to be, with sand at forty cents a ton? '

" ' Listen,' says I. ' I instruct her to keep her lamp clean and well filled. If she does that it can't burst. And with the sand in it she knows it can't, and she don't worry. It's a kind of Industrial Christian Science. She pays fifty cents, and gets both Rockefeller and Mrs. Eddy on the job. It ain't everybody that can let the gold-dust twins do their work.'

" Alfred E. Ricks all but licks the dust off of Bill Bassett's shoes.

" ' My dear young friend,' says he, ' I will never forget your generosity. Heaven will reward you. But let me implore you to turn from your ways of violence and crime.'

" ' Mousie,' says Bill, ' the hole in the wainscoting for yours. Your dogmas and inculcations sound to me like the last words of a bicycle pump. What has your high moral, elevator-service system of pillage brought you to? Penuriousness and want. Even Brother Peters, who insists upon contaminating the art of robbery with theories of commerce and trade, admitted he was on the lift. Both of you live by the gilded rule. Brother Peters,' says Bill, ' you'd better choose a slice of this embalmed currency. You're welcome.'

" I told Bill Bassett once more to put his money in his pocket. I never had the respect for burglary that some people have. I always gave something for the

money I took, even if it was only some little trifle for
a souvenir to remind 'em not to get caught again.

"And then Alfred E. Ricks grovels at Bill's feet
again, and bids us adieu. He says he will have a
team at a farmhouse, and drive to the station below,
and take the train for Denver. It salubrified the atmosphere when that lamentable boll-worm took his
departure. He was a disgrace to every non-industrial
profession in the country. With all his big schemes
and fine offices he had wound up unable even to get
an honest meal except by the kindness of a strange
and maybe unscrupulous burglar. I was glad to see
him go, though I felt a little sorry for him, now that
he was ruined forever. What could such a man do
without a big capital to work with? Why, Alfred
E. Ricks, as we left him, was as helpless as a turtle
on its back. He couldn't have worked a scheme to
beat a little girl out of a penny slate-pencil.

"When me and Bill Bassett was left alone I did a
little sleight-of mind turn in my head with a trade
secret at the end of it. Thinks I, I'll show this Mr.
Burglar Man the difference between business and labor. He had hurt some of my professional self-
adulation by casting his Persians upon commerce and
trade.

"'I won't take any of your money as a gift, Mr.

Bassett,' says I to him, ' but if you'll pay my expenses
as a traveling companion until we get out of the
danger zone of the immoral deficit you have caused in
this town's finances to-night, I'll be obliged.'

" Bill Bassett agreed to that, and we hiked westward as soon as we could catch a safe train.

" When we got to a town in Arizona called Los
Perros I suggested that we once more try our luck
on terra-cotta. That was the home of Montague Silver, my old instructor, now retired from business. I
knew Monty would stake me to web money if I could
show him a fly buzzing 'round in the locality. Bill
Bassett said all towns looked alike to him as he worked
mainly in the dark. So we got off the train in Los
Perros, a fine little town in the silver region.

" I had an elegant little sure thing in the way of a
commercial slungshot that I intended to hit Bassett
behind the ear with. I wasn't going to take his money
while he was asleep, but I was going to leave him with
a lottery ticket that would represent in experience to
him $4,755 — I think that was the amount he had
when we got off the train. But the first time I hinted
to him about an investment, he turns on me and dis-
encumbers himself of the following terms and expres-
sions.

" ' Brother Peters,' says he, ' it ain't a bad idea to

go into an enterprise of some kind, as you suggest. I think I will. But if I do it will be such a cold proposition that nobody but Robert E. Peary and Charlie Fairbanks will be able to sit on the board of directors.'

" ' I thought you might want to turn your money over,' says I.

" ' I do,' says he, ' frequently. I can't sleep on one side all night. I'll tell you, Brother Peters,' says he, ' I'm going to start a poker room. I don't seem to care for the humdrum in swindling, such as peddling egg-beaters and working off breakfast food on Barnum and Bailey for sawdust to strew in their ~~circus~~ rings. But the gambling business,' says he, ' from the profitable side of the table is a good compromise between swiping silver spoons and selling penwipers at a Waldorf-Astoria charity bazar.'

" ' Then,' says I, ' Mr. Bassett, you don't care to talk over my little business proposition? '

" Why,' says he, ' do you know, you can't get a Pasteur institute to start up within fifty miles of where I live. I bite so seldom.'

" So, Bassett rents a room over a saloon and looks around for some furniture and chromos. The same night I went to Monty Silver's house, and he let me have $200 on my prospects. Then I went to the only store in Los Perros that sold playing cards and bought every deck in the house. The next morning when the store opened I was there bringing all the cards back with me. I said that my partner that was going to back me in the game had changed his mind; and I wanted to sell the cards back again. The storekeeper took 'em at half price.

" Yes, I was seventy-five dollars loser up to that time. But while I had the cards that night I marked every one in every deck. That was labor. And then trade and commerce had their innings, and the bread I had cast upon the waters began to come back in the form of cottage pudding with wine sauce.

" Of course I was among the first to buy chips at Bill Bassett's game. He had bought the only cards there was to be had in town; and I knew the back of every one of them better than I know the back of my head when the barber shows me my haircut in the two mirrors.

" When the game closed I had the five thousand and a few odd dollars, and all Bill Bassett had was the wanderlust and a black cat he had bought for a mascot. Bill shook hands with me when I left.

" ' Brother Peters,' says he, ' I have no business being in business. I was preordained to labor. When a No. 1 burglar tries to make a James out of his jimmy he perpetrates an improfundity. You have a well-oiled and efficacious system of luck at cards,' says he. 'Peace go with you.' And I never afterward sees Bill Bassett again."

"Well, Jeff," said I, when the Autolycan adventurer seemed to have divulged the gist of his tale, "I hope you took care of the money. That would be a respecta — that is a considerable working capital if you should choose some day to settle down to some sort of regular business."

"Me?" said Jeff, virtuously. "You can bet I've taken care of that five thousand."

He tapped his coat over the region of his chest exultantly.

"Gold mining stock," he explained, "every cent of it. Shares par value one dollar. Bound to go up 500 per cent. within a year. Non-assessable. The Blue Gopher Mine. Just discovered a month ago. Better get in yourself if you've any spare dollars on hand."

"Sometimes," said I, "these mines are not —"

"Oh, this one's solid as an old goose," said Jeff. "Fifty thousand dollars' worth of ore in sight, and 10 per cent monthly earnings guaranteed."

He drew a long envelope from his pocket and cast it on the table.

"Always carry it with me," said he. "So the burglar can't corrupt or the capitalist break in and water it."

" I looked at the beautifully engraved certificate of stock.

" In Colorado, I see," said I. " And, by the way, Jeff, what was the name of the little man who went to Denver — the one you and Bill met at the station? "

" Alfred E. Ricks," said Jeff, " was the toad's designation."

" I see," said I, " the president of this mining company signs himself A. L. Fredericks. I was wondering —"

" Let me see that stock," said Jeff quickly, almost snatching it from me.

To mitigate, even though slightly, the embarrassment I summoned the waiter and ordered another bottle of the Barbera. I thought it was the least I could do.

A TEMPERED WIND

THE first time my optical nerves was disturbed by the sight of Buckingham Skinner was in Kansas City. I was standing on a corner when I see Buck stick his straw-colored head out of a third-story window of a business block and holler, " Whoa, there!   Whoa!" like you would in endeavoring to assuage a team of runaway mules.

I looked around; but all the animals I see in sight is a policeman, having his shoes shined, and a couple of delivery wagons hitched to posts.   Then in a minute downstairs tumbles this Buckingham Skinner, and runs to the corner, and stands and gazes down the other street at the imaginary dust kicked up by the fabulous hoofs of the fictitious team of chimerical quadrupeds.   And then B. Skinner goes back up to the third-story room again, and I see that the lettering on the window is " The Farmers' Friend Loan Company."

By and by Straw-top comes down again, and I crossed the street to meet him, for I had my ideas. Yes, sir, when I got close I could see where he overdone it. He was Reub all right as far as his blue jeans and cowhide boots went, but he had a matinee actor's hands, and the rye straw stuck over his ear looked like it belonged to the property man of the Old Homestead Co. Curiosity to know what his graft was got the best of me.

"Was that your team broke away and run just now?" I asks him, polite. "I tried to stop 'em," says I, "but I couldn't. I guess they're half way back to the farm by now."

"Gosh blame them darned mules," says Straw-top, in a voice so good that I nearly apologized; "they're a'lus bustin' loose." And then he looks at me close, and then he takes off his hayseed hat, and says, in a different voice: "I'd like to shake hands with Parley-voo Pickens, the greatest street man in the West, barring only Montague Silver, which you can no more than allow."

I let him shake hands with me.

"I learned under Silver," I said; "I don't begrudge him the lead. But what's your graft, son? I admit that the phantom flight of the non-existing animals at which you remarked 'Whoa!' has puzzled me somewhat. How do you win out on the trick?"

Buckingham Skinner blushed.

"Pocket money," says he; "that's all. I am tem-

porarily unfinanced. This little coup de rye straw
is good for forty dollars in a town of this size. How
do I work it? Why, I involve myself, as you perceive, in the loathsome apparel of the rural dub.
Thus embalmed I am Jonas Stubblefield — a name
impossible to improve upon. I repair noisily to the
office of some loan company conveniently located in
the third-floor, front. There I lay my hat and yarn
gloves on the floor and ask to mortgage my farm for
$2,000 to pay for my sister's musical education in
Europe. Loans like that always suit the loan com-
panies. It's ten to one that when the note falls due
the foreclosure will be leading the semiquavers by a
couple of lengths.

"Well, sir, I reach in my pocket for the abstract
of title; but I suddenly hear my team running away.
I run to the window and emit the word — or excla-
mation, which-ever it may be — viz, 'Whoa!' Then
I rush down-stairs and down the street, returning in a
few minutes. 'Dang them mules,' I says; 'they done
run away and busted the doubletree and two traces.
Now I got to hoof it home, for I never brought no
money along. Reckon we'll talk about that loan some
other time, gen'lemen.'

"Then I spreads out my tarpaulin, like the Israel-
ites, and waits for the manna to drop.

" ' Why, no, Mr. Stubblefield,' says the lobster-colored party in the specs and dotted piqué vest; ' oblige us by accepting this ten-dollar bill until to-morrow. Get your harness repaired and call in at ten. We'll be pleased to accommodate you in the matter of this loan.'

" It's a slight thing," says Buckingham Skinner, modest, " but, as I said, only for temporary loose change."

" It's nothing to be ashamed of," says I, in respect for his mortification; " in case of an emergency. Of course, it's small compared to organizing a trust or bridge whist, but even the Chicago University had to be started in a small way."

" What's your graft these days? " Buckingham Skinner asks me.

" The legitimate," says I. " I'm handling rhinestones and Dr. Oleum Sinapi's Electric Headache Battery and the Swiss Warbler's Bird Call, a small lot of the new queer ones and twos, and the Bonanza Budget, consisting of a rolled-gold wedding and engagement ring, six Egyptian lily bulbs, a combination pickle fork and nail-clipper, and fifty engraved visiting cards — no two names alike — all for the sum of 38 cents."

" Two months ago," says Buckingham Skinner. " I

was doing well down in Texas with a patent instantaneous fire kindler, made of compressed wood ashes
and benzine.   I sold loads of 'em in towns where they
like to burn niggers quick, without having to ask
somebody for a light.   And just when I was doing
the best they strikes oil down there and puts me out
of business.   ' Your machine's too slow, now, pardner,' they tells me.   ' We can have a coon in hell with
this here petroleum before your old flint-and-tinder
truck can get him warm enough to perfess religion.'
And so I gives up the kindler and drifts up here to
K. C.   This little curtain-raiser you seen me doing,
Mr. Pickens, with the simulated farm and the hypothetical team, ain't in my line at all, and I'm ashamed
you found me working it."

"No man," says I, kindly, "need to be ashamed
of putting the skibunk on a loan corporation for even
so small a sum as ten dollars, when he is financially
abashed.   Still, it wasn't quite the proper thing.   It's
too much like borrowing money without paying it
back."

I liked Buckingham Skinner from the start, for as
good a man as ever stood over the axles and breathed
gasoline smoke.   And pretty soon we gets thick, and
I let him in on a scheme I'd had in mind for some
time, and offers to go partners.

"Anything," says Buck, "that is not actually dishonest will find me willing and ready. Let us perforate into the inwardness of your proposition. I feel degraded when I am forced to wear property straw in my hair and assume a bucolic air for the small sum of ten dollars. Actually, Mr. Pickens, it makes me feel like the Ophelia of the Great Occidental All-Star One-Night Consolidated Theatrical Aggregation."

This scheme of mine was one that suited my proclivities. By nature I am some sentimental, and have always felt gentle toward the mollifying elements of existence. I am disposed to be lenient with the arts and sciences; and I find time to instigate a cordiality for the more human works of nature, such as romance and the atmosphere and grass and poetry and the Seasons. I never skin a sucker without admiring the prismatic beauty of his scales. I never sell a little auriferous trifle to the man with the hoe without noticing the beautiful harmony there is between gold and green. And that's why I liked this scheme; it was so full of outdoor air and landscapes and easy money.

We had to have a young lady assistant to help us work this graft; and I asked Buck if he knew of one to fill the bill.

" One," says I, " that is cool and wise and strictly business from her pompadour to her Oxfords. No ex-toe-dancers or gum-chewers or crayon portrait canvassers for this."

Buck claimed he knew a suitable feminine and he takes me around to see Miss Sarah Malloy. The minute I see her I am pleased. She looked to be the goods as ordered. No sign of the three p's about her — no peroxide, patchouli, nor peau de soie; about twenty-two, brown hair, pleasant ways — the kind of a lady for the place.

" A description of the sandbag, if you please," she begins.

" Why, ma'am," says I, " this graft of ours is so nice and refined and romantic, it would make the balcony scene in ' Romeo and Juliet ' look like second-story work."

We talked it over, and Miss Malloy agreed to come in as a business partner. She said she was glad to get a chance to give up her place as stenographer and secretary to a suburban lot company, and go into something respectable.

This is the way we worked our scheme. First, I figured it out by a kind of a proverb. The best grafts in the world are built up on copy-book maxims and psalms and proverbs and Esau's fables. They seem to kind of hit off human nature. Our peaceful little swindle was constructed on the old saying: " The whole push loves a lover."

One evening Buck and Miss Malloy drives up like

" She is a peach and of the cling variety."

blazes in a buggy to a farmer's door. She is pale but affectionate, clinging to his arm — always clinging to his arm. Any one can see that she is a peach

and of the cling variety. They claim they are elop-
ing for to be married on account of cruel parents.
They ask where they can find a preacher. Farmer
says, " B'gum there ain't any preacher nigher than
Reverend Abels, four miles over on Caney Creek."
Farmeress wipes her hand on her apron and rubbers
through her specs.

Then, lo and look ye! Up the road from the other
way jogs Parleyvoo Pickens in a gig, dressed in
black, white necktie, long face, sniffing his nose, emit-
ting a spurious kind of noise resembling the long
meter doxology.

" B'jinks! " says farmer, " if thar ain't a preacher
now! "

It transpires that I am Rev. Abijah Green, traveling over to Little Bethel school-house for to preach
next Sunday.

The young folks will have it they must be married,
for pa is pursuing them with the plow mules and the
buckboard. So the Reverend Green, after hesita-
tion, marries 'em in farmer's parlor. And farmer
grins, and has in cider, and says " B'gum!" and
farmeress sniffles a bit and pats the bride on the
shoulder. And Parleyvoo Pickens, the wrong reverend, writes out a marriage certificate, and farmer and
farmeress sign it as witnesses. And the parties of

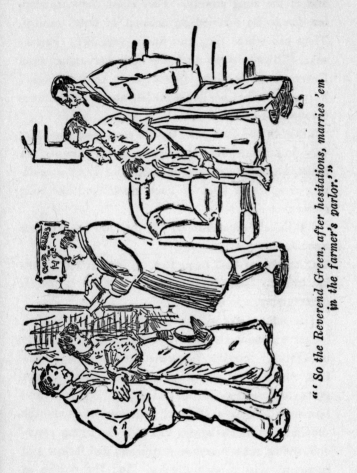

" 'So the Reverend Green, after hesitations, marries 'em in the farmer's parlor.'"

the first, second, and third part gets in their vehicles and rides away. Oh, that was an idyllic graft! True love and the lowing kine and the sun shining on the red barns — it certainly had all other impostures I know about beat to a batter.

I suppose I happened along in time to marry Buck and Miss Malloy at about twenty farm-houses. I hated to think how the romance was going to fade later on when all them marriage certificates turned up in banks where we'd discounted 'em, and the farmers had to pay them notes of hand they'd signed, running from $300 to $500.

On the 15th day of May us three divided about $6,000. Miss Malloy nearly cried with joy. You don't often see a tenderhearted girl or one that was so bent on doing right.

" Boys," says she, dabbing her eyes with a little handkerchief, " this stake comes in handier than a powder rag at a fat men's ball. It gives me a chance to reform. I was trying to get out of the real estate business when you fellows came along. But if you hadn't taken me in on this neat little proposition for removing the cuticle of the rutabaga propagators I'm afraid I'd have got into something worse. I was about to accept a place in one of these Women's Auxilary Bazars, where they build a parsonage by

"On the 15th day of May us three divided about $6,000."

selling a spoonful of chicken salad and a cream-puff
for seventy-five cents and calling it a Business Men's
Lunch.

" Now I can go into a square, honest business, and
give all them queer jobs the shake. I'm going to
Cincinnati and start a palm reading and clairvoyant
joint. As Madame Saramaloi, the Egyptian Sorcer-
ess, I shall give everybody a dollar's worth of good
honest prognostication. Good-by, boys. Take my
advice and go into some decent fake. Get friendly
with the police and newspapers and you'll be all
right."

So then we all shook hands, and Miss Malloy left
us. Me and Buck also rose up and sauntered off a
few hundred miles; for we didn't care to be around
when them marriage certificates fell due.

With about $4,000 between us we hit that bump-
tious little town off the New Jersey coast they call
New York.

If there ever was an aviary overstocked with jays
it is that Yaptown-on-the-Hudson. Cosmopolitan
they call it. You bet. So's a piece of fly-paper.
You listen close when they're buzzing and trying to
pull their feet out of the sticky stuff. " Little old
New York's good enough for us "— that's what they
sing.

There's enough Reubs walk down Broadway in one hour to buy up a week's output of the factory in Augusta, Maine, that makes Knaughty Knovelties and the little Phine Phun oroide gold finger ring that sticks a needle in your friend's hand.

You'd think New York people was all wise; but no. They don't get a chance to learn. Everything's too compressed. Even the hayseeds are baled hayseeds. But what else can you expect from a town that's shut off from the world by the ocean on one side and New Jersey on the other?

It's no place for an honest grafter with a small capital. There's too big a protective tariff on bunco. Even when Giovanni sells a quart of warm worms and chestnut hulls he has to hand out a pint to an insectivorous cop. And the hotel man charges double for everything in the bill that he sends by the patrol wagon to the altar where the duke is about to marry the heiress.

But old Badville-near-Coney is the ideal burg for a refined piece of piracy if you can pay the bunco duty. Imported grafts come pretty high. The custom-house officers that look after it carry clubs, and it's hard to smuggle in even a bib-and-tucker swindle to work Brooklyn with unless you can pay the toll. But now, me and Buck, having capital, descends upon New York to try and trade the metropolitan backwoodsmen a few glass beads for real estate just as the Vans did a hundred or two years ago.

At an East Side hotel we gets acquainted with Romulus G. Atterbury, a man with the finest head for financial operations I ever saw. It was all bald and glossy except for gray side whiskers. Seeing that head behind an office railing, and you'd deposit a million with it without a receipt. This Atterbury was well dressed, though he ate seldom; and the synopsis of his talk would make the conversation of a siren sound like a cab driver's kick. He said he used to be a member of the Stock Exchange, but some of the big capitalists got jealous and formed a ring that forced him to sell his seat.

Atterbury got to liking me and Buck and he begun to throw on the canvas for us some of the schemes that had caused his hair to evacuate. He had one scheme for starting a National Bank on $45 that made the Mississippi Bubble look as solid as a glass marble. He talked this to us for three days, and when his throat was good and sore we told him about the roll we had. Atterbury borrowed a quarter from us and went out and got a box of throat lozenges and started all over again. This time he talked bigger things, and he got us to see 'em as he did. The scheme he laid out looked like a sure winner, and he talked me and Buck into putting our capital against his burnished dome of thought. It looked all right for a kid-gloved graft. It seemed to be just about an inch and a half outside of the reach of the police, and as money-making as a mint. It was just what me and Buck wanted — a regular business at a permanent stand, with no open air spieling with tonsilitis on the street corners every evening.

So, in six weeks you see a handsome furnished set of offices down in the Wall Street neighborhood, with "The Golconda Gold Bond and Investment Company" in gilt letters on the door. And you see in his private room, with the door open, the secretary and treasurer, Mr. Buckingham Skinner, costumed like the lilies of the conservatory, with his high silk hat close to his hand. Nobody yet ever saw Buck outside of an instantaneous reach for his hat.

And you might perceive the president and general manager, Mr. R. G. Atterbury, with his priceless polished poll, busy in the main office room dictating letters to a shorthand countess, who has got pomp and a pompadour that is no less than a guarantee to investors.

There is a bookkeeper and an assistant, and a general atmosphere of varnish and culpability.

At another desk the eye is relieved by the sight of

"Busy in the main office room dictating letters to a shorthand countess."

an ordinary man, attired with unscrupulous plainness, sitting with his feet up, eating apples, with his obnoxious hat on the back of his head. That man

is no other than Colonel Tecumseh (once "Parley-
voo ") Pickens, the vice-president of the company.

"No recherché rags for me," I says to Atterbury,
when we was organizing the stage properties of the
robbery. "I'm a plain man," says I, " and I do not
use pajamas, French, or military hair-brushes. Cast
me for the rôle of the rhinestone-in-the-rough or 1
don't go on exhibition. If you can use me in my
natural, though displeasing form, do so."

"Dress you up?" says Atterbury; "I should say
not! Just as you are you're worth more to the business than a whole roomful of the things they pin
chrysanthemums on. You're to play the part of the
solid but disheveled capitalist from the Far West.
You despise the conventions. You've got so many
stocks you can afford to shake socks. Conservative,
homely, rough, shrewd, saving — that's your pose.
It's a winner in New York. Keep your feet on the
desk and eat apples. Whenever anybody comes in
eat an apple. Let 'em see you stuff the peelings in a
drawer of your desk. Look as economical and rich
and rugged as you can."

I followed out Atterbury's instructions. I played
the Rocky Mountain capitalist without ruching or
frills. The way I deposited apple peelings to my
credit in a drawer when any customers came in made

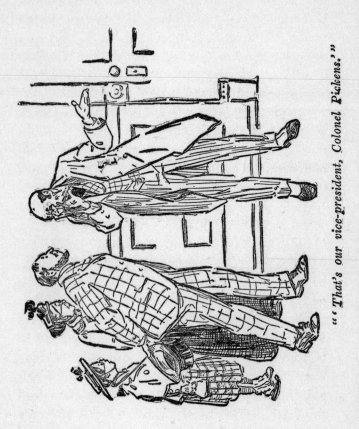

"'That's our vice-president, Colonel Pickens.'"

Hetty Green look like a spendthrift. I could hear
Atterbury saying to victims, as he smiled at me, indulgent and venerating, "That's our vice-president,
Colonel Pickens . . . fortune in Western invest-
ments . . . delightfully plain manners, but . . .
could sign his check for half a million . . . simple as
a child . . , wonderful head . . . conservative and
careful almost to a fault."

Atterbury managed the business. Me and Buck
never quite understood all of it, though he explained
it to us in full. It seems the company was a kind
of coöperative one, and everybody that bought stock
shared in the profits. First, we officers bought up a
controlling interest — we had to have that — of the
shares at 50 cents a hundred — just what the printer
charged us — and the rest went to the public at a
dollar each. The company guaranteed the stockholders a profit of ten per cent. each month, payable
on the last day thereof.

When any stockholder had paid in as much as
$100, the company issued him a Gold Bond and he
became a bondholder. I asked Atterbury one day
what benefits and appurtenances these Gold Bonds
was to an investor more so than the immunities and
privileges enjoyed by the common sucker who only
owned stock. Atterbury picked up one of them Gold

Bonds, all gilt and lettered up with flourishes and a big red seal tied with a blue ribbon in a bowknot, and he looked at me like his feelings was hurt.

"My dear Colonel Pickens," says he, "you have no soul for Art. Think of a thousand homes made happy by possessing one of these beautiful gems of the lithographer's skill! Think of the joy in the household where one of these Gold Bonds hangs by a pink cord to the what-not, or is chewed by the baby, caroling gleefully upon the floor! Ah, I see your eye growing moist, Colonel — I have touched you, have I not?"

"You have not," says I, "for I've been watching you. The moisture you see is apple juice. You can't expect one man to act as a human cider-press and an art connoisseur too."

Atterbury attended to the details of the concern. As I understand it, they was simple. The investors in stock paid in their money, and — well, I guess that's all they had to do. The company received it, and — I don't call to mind anything else. Me and Buck knew more about selling corn salve than we did about Wall Street, but even we could see how the Golconda Gold Bond Investment Company was making money. You take in money and pay back ten per cent. of it; it's plain enough that you make a clean, legitimate profit of 90 per cent., less expenses, as long as the fish bite.

Atterbury wanted to be president and treasurer too, but Buck winks an eye at him and says: "You was to furnish the brains. Do you call it good brain work when you propose to take in money at the door, too? Think again. I hereby nominate myself treasurer ad valorem, sine die, and by acclamation. I chip in that much brain work free. Me and Pickens, we furnished the capital, and we'll handle the unearned increment as it incremates."

It costs us $500 for office rent and first payment on furniture; $1,500 more went for printing and advertising. Atterbury knew his business. "Three months to a minute we'll last," says he. "A day longer than that and we'll have to either go under or go under an alias. By that time we ought to clean up $60,000. And then a money belt and a lower berth for me, and the yellow journals and the furniture men can pick the bones."

Our ads. done the work. "Country weeklies and Washington hand-press dailies of course," says I when we was ready to make contracts.

"Man," says Atterbury, "as its advertising manager you would cause a Limburger cheese factory to remain undiscovered during a hot summer. The game we're after is right here in New York and Brooklyn and the Harlem reading-rooms. They're the people that the street-car fenders and the Answers to Correspondents columns and the pickpocket notices are made for. We want our ads. in the biggest city dailies, top of column, next to editorials on radium and pictures of the girl doing health exercises."

Pretty soon the money begins to roll in. Buck didn't have to pretend to be busy; his desk was piled high up with money orders and checks and greenbacks. People began to drop in the office and buy stock every day.

Most of the shares went in small amounts — $10 and $25 and $50, and a good many $2 and $3 lots. And the bald and inviolate cranium of President Atterbury shines with enthusiasm and demerit, while Colonel Tecumseh Pickens, the rude but reputable Crœsus of the West, consumes so many apples that the peelings hang to the floor from the mahogany garbage chest that he calls his desk.

Just as Atterbury said, we ran along about three months without being troubled. Buck cashed the paper as fast as it came in and kept the money in a safe deposit vault a block or so away. Buck never thought much of banks for such purposes. We paid

the interest regular on the stock we'd sold, so there
was nothing for anybody to squeal about. We had
nearly $50,000 on hand and all three of us had been
living as high as prize fighters out of training.

One morning, as me and Buck sauntered into the
office, fat and flippant, from our noon grub, we met
an easy-looking fellow, with a bright eye and a pipe
in his mouth, coming out. We found Atterbury
looking like he'd been caught a mile from home in a
wet shower.

" Know that man? " he asked us.

We said we didn't.

" I don't either," says Atterbury, wiping off his
head; " but I'll bet enough Gold Bonds to paper a
cell in the Tombs that he's a newspaper reporter."

" What did he want? " asks Buck.

" Information," says our president. " Said he
was thinking of buying some stock. He asked me
about nine hundred questions, and every one of 'em
hit some sore place in the business. I know he's on a
paper. You can't fool me. You see a man about
half shabby, with an eye like a gimlet, smoking cut
plug, with dandruff on his coat collar, and knowing
more than J. P. Morgan and Shakespeare put together — if that ain't a reporter I never saw one. I
was afraid of this. I don't mind detectives and post-

office inspectors — I talk to 'em eight minutes and then sell 'em stock — but them reporters take the starch out of my collar.   Boys, I recommend that we declare a dividend and fade away.   The signs point that way."

Me and Buck talked to Atterbury and got him to stop sweating and stand still.   That fellow didn't look like a reporter to us.   Reporters always pull out a pencil and tablet on you, and tell you a story you've heard, and strike you for the drinks.   But Atterbury was shaky and nervous all day.

The next day me and Buck comes down from the hotel about ten-thirty.   On the way we buys the papers, and the first thing we see is a column on the front page about our little imposition.   It was a shame the way that reporter intimated that we were no blood relatives of the late George W. Childs.   He tells all about the scheme as he sees it, in a rich, racy kind of a guying style that might amuse most any-body except a stockholder.   Yes, Atterbury was right; it behooveth the gaily clad treasurer and the pearly pated president and the rugged vice-president of the Golconda Gold Bond and Investment Company to go away real sudden and quick that their days might be longer upon the land.

Me and Buck hurries down to the office.   We finds

on the stairs and in the hall a crowd of people trying
)to squeeze into our office, which is already jammed
'full inside to the railing. They're nearly all got
Golconda stock and Gold Bonds in their hands. Me
and Buck judged they'd been reading the papers,
too.

We stopped and looked at our stockholders, some
surprised. It wasn't quite the kind of a gang we
supposed had been investing. They all looked like
poor people; there was plenty of old women and lots
of young girls that you'd say worked in factories and
mills. Some was old men that looked like war vet-
erans, and some was crippled, and a good many was
just kids — bootblacks and newsboys and messen-
gers. Some was working-men in overalls, with their
sleeves rolled up. Not one of the gang looked like a
stockholder in anything unless it was a peanut stand.
But they all had Golconda stock and looked as sick
as you please.

I saw a queer kind of a pale look come on Buck's
face when he sized up the crowd. He stepped up to
a sickly looking woman and says: "Madam, do you
own any of this stock?"

"I put in a hundred dollars," says the woman,
faint like. "It was all I had saved in a year. One
of my children is dying at home now and I haven't a

"But they all had Golconda stock and looked as sick as you please."

cent in the house. I came to see if I could draw out some. The circulars said you could draw it at any time. But they say now I will lose it all."

There was a smart kind of a kid in the gang — I guess he was a newsboy. "I got in twenty-fi', mister," he says, looking hopeful at Buck's silk hat and clothes. "Dey paid me two-fifty a mont' on it. Say, a man tells me dey can't do dat and be on de square. Is dat straight? Do you guess I can get out my twent-fi'?"

Some of the old women was crying. The factory girls was plumb distracted. They'd lost all their savings and they'd be docked for the time they lost coming to see about it.

There was one girl — a pretty one — in a red shawl, crying in a corner like her heart would dissolve. Buck goes over and asks her about it.

"It ain't so much losing the money, mister," says she, shaking all over, "though I've been two years saving it up; but Jakey won't marry me now. He'll take Rosa Steinfeld. I know J — J — Jakey. She's got $400 in the savings bank. Ai, ai, ai —" she sings out.

Buck looks all around with that same funny look on his face. And then we see leaning against the wall, puffing at his pipe, with his eye shining at us, this newspaper reporter.   Buck and me walks over to him.

"You're a real interesting writer," says Buck.

"'Jakey won't marry me now.   He'll take Rosa Steinfield.'"

"How far do you mean to carry it?   Anything more up your sleeve?"

"Oh, I'm just waiting around," says the reporter.

smoking away, " in case any news turns up. It's up
to your stockholders now. Some of them might com-
plain, you know. Isn't that the patrol wagon
now? " he says, listening to a sound outside. " No,"
he goes on, " that's Doc. Whittleford's old cadaver
coupé from the Roosevelt. I ought to know that
gong. Yes, I suppose I've written some interesting
stuff at times."

" You wait," says Buck; " I'm going to throw an
item of news in your way."

Buck reaches in his pocket and hands me a key.
I knew what he meant before he spoke. Confounded
old buccaneer — I knew what he meant. They don't
make them any better than Buck.

" Pick," says he, looking at me hard, " ain't this
graft a little out of our line? Do we want Jakey
to marry Rosa Steinfeld? "

" You've got my vote," says I. " I'll have it here
in ten minutes." And I starts for the safe deposit
vaults.

I comes back with the money done up in a big
bundle, and then Buck and me takes the journalist
reporter around to another door and we let ourselves
into one of the office rooms.

" Now, my literary friend," says Buck, " take a
chair, and keep still, and I'll give you an interview.

You see before you two grafters from Graftersville, Grafter County, Arkansas. Me and Pick have sold brass jewelry, hair tonic, song books, marked cards, patent medicines, Connecticut Smyrna rugs, furniture polish, and albums in every town from Old Point Comfort to the Golden Gate. We've grafted a dollar whenever we saw one that had a surplus look to it. But we never went after the simoleon in the toe of the sock under the loose brick in the corner of the kitchen hearth. There's an old saying you may have heard —'fussily decency averni'—which means it's an easy slide from the street faker's dry goods box to a desk in Wall Street. We've took that slide, but we didn't know exactly what was at the bottom of it. Now, you ought to be wise, but you ain't. You've got New York wiseness, which means that you judge a man by the outside of his clothes. That ain't right. You ought to look at the lining and seams and the button-holes. While we are waiting for the patrol wagon you might get out your little stub pencil and take notes for another funny piece in the paper."

And then Buck turns to me and says: "I don't care what Atterbury thinks. He only put in brains, and if he gets his capital out he's lucky. But what do you say, Pick?"

"Me?" says I. "You ought to know me, Buck. I didn't know who was buying the stock."

"All right," says Buck. And then he goes through the inside door into the main office and looks at the gang trying to squeeze through the railing. Atterbury and his hat was gone. And Buck makes 'em a short speech.

"All you lambs get in line. You're going to get your wool back. Don't shove so. Get in a line — a *line* — not in a pile. Lady, will you please stop bleating? Your money's waiting for you. Here, sonny, don't climb over that railing; your dimes are safe. Don't cry, sis; you ain't out a cent. Get in *line*, I say. Here, Pick, come and straighten 'em out and let 'em through and out by the other door."

Buck takes off his coat, pushes his silk hat on the back of his head, and lights up a reina victoria. He sets at the table with the boodle before him, all done up in neat packages. I gets the stockholders strung out and marches 'em, single file, through from the main room; and the reporter man passes 'em out of the side door into the hall again. As they go by, Buck takes up the stock and the Gold Bonds, paying 'em cash, dollar for dollar, the same as they paid in.

The shareholders of the Golconda Gold Bond and Investment Company can't hardly believe it. They

"The shareholders of the Golconda Gold Bond and Investment Company can't hardly believe it"

almost grabs the money out of Buck's hands. Some of the women keep on crying, for it's a custom of the sex to cry when they have sorrow, to weep when they have joy, and to shed tears whenever they find them-selves without either.

The old women's fingers shake when they stuff the skads in the bosom of their rusty dresses. The fac-tory girls just stoop over and flap their dry goods a second, and you hear the elastic go " pop " as the currency goes down in the ladies' department of the " Old Domestic Lisle-Thread Bank."

Some of the stockholders that had been doing the Jeremiah act the loudest outside had spasms of re-stored confidence and wanted to leave the money in-vested. " Salt away that chicken feed in your duds, and skip along," says Buck. " What business have you got investing in bonds? The tea-pot or the crack in the wall behind the clock for your hoard of pennies."

When the pretty girl in the red shawl cashes in Buck hands her an extra twenty.

" A wedding present," says our treasurer, " from the Golconda Company. And say — if Jakey ever follows his nose, even at a respectful distance, around the corner where Rosa Steinfeld lives, you are hereby authorized to knock a couple of inches of it off."

When they was all paid off and gone, Buck calls the newspaper reporter and shoves the rest of the money over to him.

"You begun this," says Buck; "now finish it. Over there are the books, showing every share and bond issued. Here's the money to cover, except what we've spent to live on. You'll have to act as receiver. I guess you'll do the square thing on account of your paper. This is the best way we know how to settle it. Me and our substantial but apple-weary vice-president are going to follow the example of our revered president, and skip. Now, have you got enough news for to-day, or do you want to interview us on etiquette and the best way to make over an old taffeta skirt?"

"News!" says the newspaper man, taking his pipe out; "do you think I could use this? I don't want to lose my job. Suppose I go around to the office and tell 'em this happened. What'll the managing editor say? He'll just hand me a pass to Bellevue and tell me to come back when I get cured. I might turn in a story about a sea serpent wiggling up Broadway, but I haven't got the nerve to try 'em with a pipe like this. A get-rich-quick — excuse me — gang giving back the boodle! Oh, no. I'm not on the comic supplement."

"You can't understand it, of course," says Buck, with his hand on the door knob. "Me and Pick ain't Wall Streeters like you know 'em. We never allowed to swindle sick old women and working girls and take nickels off of kids. In the lines of graft we've worked we took money from the people the Lord made to be buncoed — sports and rounders and smart Alecks and street crowds, that always have a few dollars to throw away, and farmers that wouldn't ever be happy if the grafters didn't come around and play with 'em when they sold their crops. We never cared to fish for the kind of suckers that bite here. No, sir. We got too much respect for the profession and for ourselves. Good-by to you, Mr. Receiver."

"Here!" says the journalist reporter; "wait a minute. There's a broker I know on the next floor. Wait till I put this truck in his safe. I want you fellows to take a drink on me before you go."

"On you?" says Buck, winking solemn. "Don't you go and try to make 'em believe at the office you said that. Thanks. We can't spare the time, I reckon. So long."

And me and Buck slides out the door; and that's the way the Golconda Company went into involuntary liquefaction.

If you had seen me and Buck the next night you'd have had to go to a little bum hotel over near the West Side ferry landings. We was in a little back room, and I was filling up a gross of six-ounce bottles with hydrant water colored red with aniline and flavored with cinnamon. Buck was smoking, contented, and he wore a decent brown derby in place of his silk hat.

"It's a good thing, Pick," says he, as he drove in the corks, "that we got Brady to loan us his horse and wagon for a week. We'll rustle up a stake by then. This hair tonic'll sell right along over in Jersey. Bald heads ain't popular over there on account of the mosquitoes."

Directly I dragged out my valise and went down in it for labels.

"Hair tonic labels are out," says I. "Only about a dozen on hand."

"Buy some more," says Buck.

We investigated our pockets and found we had just enough money to settle our hotel bill in the morning and pay our passage over the ferry.

"Plenty of the 'Shake-the-Shakes Chill Cure' labels," says I, after looking.

"What more do you want?" says Buck. "Slap 'em on. The chill season is just opening up in the

Hackensack low grounds. What's hair, anyway, if you have to shake it off?"

We posted on the Chill Cure labels about half an hour and Buck says:

"Making an honest livin's better than that Wall Street, anyhow; ain't it, Pick?"

"You bet," says I.

HOSTAGES TO MOMUS

I

1 NEVER got inside of the legitimate line of graft
but once. But, one time, as I say, I reversed the decision of the revised statutes and undertook a thing
that I'd have to apologize for even under the New
Jersey trust laws.

Me and Caligula Polk, of Muskogee in the Creek
Nation, was down in the Mexican State of Tamauli-
pas running a peripatetic lottery and monte game.
Now, selling lottery tickets is a government graft
in Mexico, just like selling forty-eight cents' worth
of postage-stamps for forty-nine cents is over here.
So Uncle Porfirio he instructs the *rurales* to attend to
our case.

Rurales? They're a sort of country police; but
don't draw any mental crayon portraits of the
worthy constable with a tin star and a gray goatee.
The *rurales* — well, if we'd mount our Supreme
Court on broncos, arm 'em with Winchesters, and
start 'em out after John Doe *et al.,* we'd have about
the same thing.

When the *rurales* started for us we started for the States. They chased us as far as Matamoras. We hid in a brickyard; and that night we swum the Rio Grande, Caligula with a brick in each hand, absentminded, which he drops upon the soil of Texas, forgetting he had 'em.

From there we emigrated to San Antone, and then over to New Orleans, where we took a rest. And in that town of cotton bales and other adjuncts to female beauty we made the acquaintance of drinks invented by the Creoles during the period of Louey Cans, in which they are still served at the side doors. The most I can remember of this town is that me and Caligula and a Frenchman named McCarty — wait a minute; Adolph McCarty — was trying to make the French Quarter pay up the back trading-stamps due on the Louisiana Purchase, when somebody hollers that the johndarms are coming. I have an insufficient recollection of buying two yellow tickets through a window; and I seemed to see a man swing a lantern and say "All aboard!" I remembered no more, except that the train butcher was covering me and Caligula up with Augusta J. Evans's works and figs.

When we become revised, we find that we have collided up against the State of Georgia at a spot hitherto unaccounted for in time tables except by an asterisk, which means that trains stop every other Thursday on signal by tearing up a rail. We was waked up in a yellow pine hotel by the noise of flowers and the smell of birds. Yes, sir, for the wind was banging sunflowers as big as buggy wheels against the weatherboarding and the chicken coop was right under the window. Me and Caligula dressed and went down-stairs. The landlord was shelling peas on the front porch. He was six feet of chills and fever, and Hongkong in complexion, though in other respects he seemed amenable in the exercise of his sentiments and features.

Caligula, who is a spokesman by birth, and a small man, though red-haired and impatient of painfulness of any kind, speaks up.

"Pardner," says he, "good-morning, and be darned to you. Would you mind telling us why we are at? We know the reason we are where, but can't exactly figure out on account of at what place."

"Well, gentlemen," says the landlord, "I reckoned you-all would be inquiring this morning. You-all dropped off of the nine thirty train here last night; and you was right tight. Yes, you was right smart in liquor. I can inform you that you are now in the town of Mountain Valley, in the State of Georgia."

" On top of that," says Caligula, " don't say that we can't have anything to eat."

" Sit down, gentlemen," says the landlord, " and in twenty minutes I'll call you to the best breakfast you can get anywhere in town."

That breakfast turned out to be composed of fried bacon and a yellowish edifice that proved up something between pound cake and flexible sandstone. The landlord calls it corn pone; and then he sets out a dish of the exaggerated breakfast food known as hominy; and so me and Caligula makes the acquaintance of the celebrated food that enabled every Johnny Reb to lick one and two-thirds Yankees for nearly four years at a stretch.

" The wonder to me is," says Caligula, " that Uncle Robert Lee's boys didn't chase the Grant and Sherman outfit clear up into Hudson's Bay. It would have made me that mad to eat this truck they call mahogany!"

" Hog and hominy," I explains, " is the staple food of this section."

" Then," says Caligula, " they ought to keep it where it belongs. I thought this was a hotel and not a stable. Now, if we was in Muskogee at the St.

Lucifer House, I'd show you some breakfast grub. Antelope steaks and fried liver to begin on, and venison cutlets with *chili con carne* and pineapple fritters, and then some sardines and mixed pickles; and top it off with a can of yellow clings and a bottle of beer. You won't find a layout like that on the bill of affairs of any of your Eastern restauraws."

"Too lavish," says I. "I've traveled, and I'm unprejudiced. There'll never be a perfect breakfast eaten until some man grows arms long enough to stretch down to New Orleans for his coffee and over to Norfolk for his rolls, and reaches up to Vermont and digs a slice of butter out of a spring-house, and then turns over a beehive close to a white clover patch out in Indiana for the rest. Then he'd come pretty close to making a meal on the amber that the gods eat on Mount Olympia."

"Too ephemeral," says Caligula. "I'd want ham and eggs, or rabbit stew, anyhow, for a chaser. What do you consider the most edifying and casual in the way of a dinner?"

"I've been infatuated from time to time," I answers, "with fancy ramifications of grub such as terrapins, lobsters, reed birds, jambolaya, and canvas-covered ducks; but after all there's nothing less displeasing to me than a beefsteak smothered in mushrooms on a balcony in sound of the Broadway street-cars, with a hand-organ playing down below, and the boys hollering extras about the latest suicide. For the wine, give me a reasonable Ponty Cany. And that's all, except a *demi-tasse*."

"Well," says Caligula, "I reckon in New York you get to be a conniseer; and when you go around with the *demi-tasse* you are naturally bound to buy 'em stylish grub."

"It's a great town for epicures," says I. "You'd soon fall into their ways if you was there."

"I've heard it was," says Caligula. "But I reckon I wouldn't. I can polish my fingernails all they need myself."

II

After breakfast we went out on the front porch, lighted up two of the landlord's *flor de upas* perfectos, and took a look at Georgia.

The installment of scenery visible to the eye looked mighty poor. As far as we could see was red hills all washed down with gullies and scattered over with patches of piny woods. Blackberry bushes was all that kept the rail fences from falling down. About fifteen miles over to the north was a little range of well-timbered mountains.

That town of Mountain Valley wasn't going. About a dozen people permeated along the sidewalks; but what you saw mostly was rain-barrels and roosters, and boys poking around with sticks in piles of ashes made by burning the scenery of Uncle Tom shows.

And just then there passes down on the other side of the street a high man in a long black coat and a beaver hat. All the people in sight bowed, and some crossed the street to shake hands with him; folks came out of stores and houses to holler at him; women leaned out of windows and smiled; and all the kids stopped playing to look at him. Our landlord stepped out on the porch and bent himself double like a carpenter's rule, and sung out, " Good-morning, Colonel," when he was a dozen yards gone by.

" And is that Alexander, pa? " says Caligula to the landlord; " and why is he called great? "

" That, gentlemen," says the landlord, " is no less than Colonel Jackson T. Rockingham, the president of the Sunrise & Edenville Tap Railroad, mayor of Mountain Valley, and chairman of the Perry County board of immigration and public improvements."

" Been away a good many years, hasn't he? " I asked.

" No, sir; Colonel Rockingham is going down to
the post-office for his mail. His fellow-citizens take
pleasure in greeting him thus every morning. The
colonel is our most prominent citizen. Besides the
height of the stock of the Sunrise & Edenville Tap
Railroad, he owns a thousand acres of that land
across the creek. Mountain Valley delights, sir, to
honor a citizen of such worth and public spirit."

For an hour that afternoon Caligula sat on the
back of his neck on the porch and studied a newspaper, which was unusual in a man who despised
print. When he was through he took me to the end
of the porch among the sunlight and drying dish-
towels. I knew that Caligula had invented a new
graft. For he chewed the ends of his mustache and
ran the left catch of his suspenders up and down,
which was his way.

" What is it now? " I asks. " Just so it ain't
floating mining stocks or raising Pennsylvania pinks,
we'll talk it over."

" Pennsylvania pinks? Oh, that refers to a coin-
raising scheme of the Keystoners. They burn the
soles of old women's feet to make them tell where
their money's hid."

Caligula's words in business was always few and
bitter.

" You see them mountains," said he, pointing. " And you seen that colonel man that owns railroads and cuts more ice when he goes to the post-office than Roosevelt does when he cleans 'em out. What we're going to do is to kidnap the latter into the former, and inflict a ransom of ten thousand dollars."

" Illegality," says I, shaking my head.

" I knew you'd say that," says Caligula. " At first sight it does seem to jar peace and dignity. But it don't. I got the idea out of that newspaper. Would you commit aspersions on a equitable graft that the United States itself has condoned and indorsed and ratified? "

" Kidnapping," says I, " is an immoral function in the derogatory list of the statutes. If the United States upholds it, it must be a recent enactment of ethics, along with race suicide and rural delivery."

" Listen," says Caligula, " and I'll explain the case set down in the papers. Here was a Greek citizen named Burdick Harris," says he, " captured for a graft by Africans; and the United States sends two gunboats to the State of Tangiers and makes the King of Morocco give up seventy thousand dollars to Raisuli."

" Go slow," says I. " That sounds too international to take in all at once. It's like ' thimble, thimble, who's got the naturalization papers? ' "

" 'Twas press despatches from Constantinople," says Caligula. " You'll see, six months from now. They'll be confirmed by the monthly magazines; and then it won't be long till you'll notice 'em alongside of photos of the Mount Pelee eruption photos in the while-you-get-your-hair-cut-weeklies. It's all right, Pick. This African man Raisuli hides Burdick Harris up in the mountains, and advertises his price to the governments of different nations. Now, you wouldn't think for a minute," goes on Caligula, " that John Hay would have chipped in and helped this graft along if it wasn't a square game, would you? "

" Why, no," says I. " I've always stood right in with Bryan's policies, and I couldn't consciously say a word against the Republican administration just now. But if Harris was a Greek, on what system of international protocols did Hay interfere? "

" It ain't exactly set forth in the papers," says Caligula. " I suppose it's a matter of sentiment. You know he wrote this poem, ' Little Breeches '; and them Greeks wear little or none. But anyhow, John Hay sends the Brooklyn and the Olympia over,

and they cover Africa with thirty-inch guns. And
then Hay cables after the health of the *persona
grata.* 'And how are they this morning?' he wires.
'Is Burdick Harris alive yet, or Mr. Raisuli dead?'
And the King of Morocco sends up the seventy
thousand dollars, and they turn Burdick Harris
loose. And there's not half the hard feelings among
the nations about this little kidnapping matter as
there was about the peace congress. And Burdick
Harris says to the reporters, in the Greek language,
that he's often heard about the United States, and
he admires Roosevelt next to Raisuli, who is one of
the whitest and most gentlemanly kidnappers that he
ever worked alongside of. So you see, Pick," winds
up Caligula, " we've got the law of nations on our
side. We'll cut this colonel man out of the herd, and
corral him in them little mountains, and stick up his
heirs and assigns for ten thousand dollars."

"Well, you seldom little red-headed territorial ter-
ror," I answers, " you can't bluff your uncle Tecumseh Pickens! I'll be your company in this graft.
But I misdoubt if you've absorbed the inwardness of
this Burdick Harris case, Calig; and if on any morning we get a telegram from the Secretary of State
asking about the health of the scheme, I propose to
acquire the most propinquitous and celeritous mule in

this section and gallop diplomatically over into the neighboring and peaceful nation of Alabama."

III

Me and Caligula spent the next three days investigating the bunch of mountains into which we proposed to kidnap Colonel Jackson T. Rockingham. We finally selected an upright slice of topography, covered with bushes and trees that you could only reach by a secret path that we cut out up the side of it. And the only way to reach the mountain was to follow up the bend of a branch that wound among the elevations.

Then I took in hand an important subdivision of the proceedings. I went up to Atlanta on the train and laid in a two-hundred-and-fifty-dollar supply of the most gratifying and efficient lines of grub that money could buy. I always was an admirer of viands in their more palliative and revised stages. Hog and hominy are not only inartistic to my stomach, but they give indigestion to my moral sentiments. And I thought of Colonel Jackson T. Rockingham, president of the Sunrise & Edenville Tap Railroad, and how he would miss the luxury of his home fare as is so famous among wealthy Southern-

ers. So I sunk half of mine and Caligula's capital
in as elegant a layout of fresh and canned provisions
as Burdick Harris or any other professional kid-
nappee ever saw in a camp.

I put another hundred in a couple of cases of Bor-
deaux, two quarts of cognac, two hundred Havana
regalias with gold bands, and a camp stove and stools
and folding cots. I wanted Colonel Rockingham to
be comfortable; and I hoped after he gave up the
ten thousand dollars he would give me and Caligula
as good a name for gentlemen and entertainers as
the Greek man did the friend of his that made the
United States his bill collector against Africa.

When the goods came down from Atlanta, we hired
a wagon, moved them up on the little mountain, and
established camp. And then we laid for the colonel.

We caught him one morning about two miles out
from Mountain Valley, on his way to look after some
of his burnt umber farm land. He was an elegant
old gentleman, as thin and tall as a trout rod, with
frazzled shirt-cuffs and specs on a black string. We
explained to him, brief and easy, what we wanted;
and Caligula showed him, careless, the handle of his
forty-five under his coat.

"What?" says Colonel Rockingham. "Bandits
in Perry County, Georgia! I shall see that the

board of immigration and public improvements hears of this!"

"Be so unfoolhardy as to climb into that buggy," says Caligula, "by order of the board of perforation and public depravity. This is a business meeting, and we're anxious to adjourn *sine qua non.*"

We drove Colonel Rockingham over the mountain and up the side of it as far as the buggy could go. Then we tied the horse, and took our prisoner on foot up to the camp.

"Now, colonel," I says to him, "we're after the ransom, me and my partner; and no harm will come to you if the King of Mor — if your friends send up the dust. In the mean time we are gentlemen the same as you. And if you give us your word not to try to escape, the freedom of the camp is yours."

"I give you my word," says the colonel.

"All right," says I; "and now it's eleven o'clock, and me and Mr. Polk will proceed to inoculate the occasion with a few well-timed trivialities in the line of grub."

"Thank you," says the colonel; "I believe I could relish a slice of bacon and a plate of hominy."

"But you won't," says I emphatic. "Not in this camp. We soar in higher regions than them occupied by your celebrated but repulsive dish."

While the colonel read his paper, me and Caligula took off our coats and went in for a little luncheon *de luxe* just to show him. Caligula was a fine cook of the Western brand. He could toast a buffalo or fricassee a couple of steers as easy as a woman could make a cup of tea. He was gifted in the way of knocking together edibles when haste and muscle and quantity was to be considered. He held the record west of the Arkansas River for frying pancakes with his left hand, broiling venison cutlets with his right, and skinning a rabbit with his teeth at the same time. But I could do things *en casserole* and *à la creole*, and handle the oil and tobasco as gently and nicely as a French *chef*.

So at twelve o'clock we had a hot lunch ready that looked like a banquet on a Mississippi River steamboat. We spread it on the tops of two or three big boxes, opened two quarts of the red wine, set the olives and a canned oyster cocktail and a ready-made Martini by the colonel's plate, and called him to grub.

Colonel Rockingham drew up his campstool, wiped off his specs, and looked at the things on the table. Then I thought he was swearing; and I felt mean because I hadn't taken more pains with the victuals. But he wasn't; he was asking a blessing; and me and

Caligula hung our heads, and I saw a tear drop from the colonel's eye into his cocktail.

I never saw a man eat with so much earnestness and application — not hastily, like a grammarian, or one of the canal, but slow and appreciative, like a anaconda, or a real *vive bonjour*.

In an hour and a half the colonel leaned back. I brought him a pony of brandy and his black coffee, and set the box of Havana regalias on the table.

" Gentlemen," says he, blowing out the smoke and trying to breathe it back again, " when we view the eternal hills and the smiling and beneficent landscape, and reflect upon the goodness of the Creator who —"

" Excuse me, colonel," says I, " but there's some business to attend to now "; and I brought out paper and pen and ink and laid 'em before him. " Who do you want to send to for the money? " I asks.

" I reckon," says he, after thinking a bit, " to the vice-president of our railroad, at the general offices of the Company in Edenville."

" How far is it to Edenville from here? " I asked.

" About ten miles," says he.

Then I dictated these lines, and Colonel Rockingham wrote them out:

I am kidnapped and held a prisoner by two desperate outlaws in a place which is useless to attempt to find. They demand ten thousand dollars at once for my release. The amount must be raised immediately, and these directions followed. Come alone with the money to Stony Creek, which runs out of Blacktop Mountains. Follow the bed of the creek till you come to a big flat rock on the left bank, on which is marked a cross in red chalk. Stand on the rock and wave a white flag. A guide will come to you and conduct you to where I am held. Lose no time.

After the colonel had finished this, he asked permission to tack on a postscript about how white he was being treated, so the railroad wouldn't feel uneasy in its bosom about him. We agreed to that. He wrote down that he had just had lunch with the two desperate ruffians; and then he set down the whole bill of fare, from cocktails to coffee. He wound up with the remark that dinner would be ready about six, and would probably be a more licentious and intemperate affair than lunch.

Me and Caligula read it, and decided to let it go; for we, being cooks, were amenable to praise, though it sounded out of place on a sight draft for ten thousand dollars.

I took the letter over to the Mountain Valley road and watched for a messenger. By and by a colored equestrian came along on horseback, riding toward Edenville. I gave him a dollar to take the letter to the railroad offices; and then I went back to camp.

IV

About four o'clock in the afternoon, Caligula, who was acting as lookout, calls to me:

"I have to report a white shirt signaling on the starboard bow, sir."

I went down the mountain and brought back a fat, red man in an alpaca coat and no collar.

"Gentlemen," says Colonel Rockingham, "allow me to introduce my brother, Captain Duval C. Rockingham, vice-president of the Sunrise & Edenville Tap Railroad."

"Otherwise the King of Morocco," says I. "I reckon you don't mind my counting the ransom, just as a business formality."

"Well, no, not exactly," says the fat man, "not when it comes. I turned that matter over to our second vice-president. I was anxious after Brother Jackson's safetiness. I reckon he'll be along right soon. What does that lobster salad you mentioned taste like, Brother Jackson?"

"Mr. Vice-President," says I, "you'll oblige us by remaining here till the second V. P. arrives. This is a private rehearsal, and we don't want any roadside speculators selling tickets."

In half an hour Caligula sings out again:

" Sail ho ! Looks like an apron on a broomstick."

I perambulated down the cliff again, and escorted up a man six foot three, with a sandy beard and no other dimensions that you could notice. Thinks I to myself, if he's got ten thousand dollars on his person it's in one bill and folded lengthwise.

" Mr. Patterson G. Coble, our second vice-president," announces the colonel.

" Glad to know you, gentlemen," says this Coble. " I came up to disseminate the tidings that Major Tallahassee Tucker, our general passenger agent, is now negotiating a peachcrate full of our railroad bonds with the Perry County Bank for a loan. My dear Colonel Rockingham, was that chicken gumbo or cracked goobers on the bill of fare in your note? Me and the conductor of fifty-six was having a dispute about it."

" Another white wings on the rocks ! " hollers Caligula. " If I see any more I'll fire on 'em and swear they was torpedo-boats ! "

The guide goes down again, and convoys into the lair a person in blue overalls carrying an amount of inebriety and a lantern. I am so sure that this is Major Tucker that I don't even ask him until we are up above; and then I discover that it is Uncle Timothy, the yard switchman at Edenville, who is sent

ahead to flag our understandings with the gossip that
Judge Pendergast, the railroad's attorney, is in the
process of mortgaging Colonel Rockingham's farming lands to make up the ransom.

While he is talking, two men crawl from under the
bushes into camp, and Caligula, with no white flag to
disinter him from his plain duty, draws his gun. But
again Colonel Rockingham intervenes and introduces
Mr. Jones and Mr. Batts, engineer and fireman of
train number forty-two.

"Excuse us," says Batts, "but me and Jim have
hunted squirrels all over this mounting, and we don't
need no white flag. Was that straight, colonel, about
the plum pudding and pineapples and real store ci-
gars?"

"Towel on a fishing-pole in the offing!" howls
Caligula. "Suppose it's the firing line of the freight
conductors and brakeman."

"My last trip down," says I, wiping off my face.
"If the S. & E. T. wants to run an excursion up
here just because we kidnapped their president, let
'em. We'll put out our sign. 'The Kidnapper's
Cafe and Trainmen's Home.'"

This time I caught Major Tallahassee Tucker by
his own confession, and I felt easier. I asked him
into the creek, so I could drown him if he happened

to be a track-walker or caboose porter. All the way up the mountain he driveled to me about asparagus on toast, a thing that his intelligence in life had skipped.

Up above I got his mind segregated from food and asked if he had raised the ransom.

"My dear sir," says he, "I succeeded in negotiating a loan on thirty thousand dollars' worth of the bonds of our railroad, and —"

"Never mind just now, major," says I. "It's all right, then. Wait till after dinner, and we'll settle the business. All of you gentlemen," I continues to the crowd, "are invited to stay to dinner. We have mutually trusted one another, and the white flag is supposed to wave over the proceedings."

"The correct idea," says Caligula, who was standing by me. "Two baggage-masters and a ticket-agent dropped out of a tree while you was below the last time. Did the major man bring the money?"

"He says," I answered, "that he succeeded in negotiating the loan."

If any cooks ever earned ten thousand dollars in twelve hours, me and Caligula did that day. At six o'clock we spread the top of the mountain with as fine a dinner as the personnel of any railroad ever engulfed. We opened all the wine, and we concocted entrées and *pièces de resistance*, and stirred up little

savory *chef de cuisines* and organized a mass of grub
such as has been seldom instigated out of canned and
bottled goods. The railroad gathered around it, and
the wassail and diversions was intense.

After the feast me and Caligula, in the line of
business, takes Major Tucker to one side and talks
ransom. The major pulls out an agglomeration of
currency about the size of the price of a town lot
in the suburbs of Rabbitville, Arizona, and makes
this outcry.

"Gentlemen," says he, "the stock of the Sunrise
& Edenville railroad has depreciated some. The best
I could do with thirty thousand dollars' worth of the
bonds was to secure a loan of eighty-seven dollars and
fifty cents. On the farming lands of Colonel Rockingham, Judge Pendergast was able to obtain, on a
ninth mortgage, the sum of fifty dollars. You will
find the amount, one hundred and thirty-seven fifty,
correct."

"A railroad president," said I, looking this Tucker
in the eye, "and the owner of a thousand acres of
land; and yet —"

"Gentlemen," says Tucker, "The railroad is ten
miles long. There don't any train run on it except
when the crew goes out in the pines and gathers
enough lightwood knots to get up steam. A long

time ago, when times was good, the net earnings used to run as high as eighteen dollars a week. Colonel Rockingham's land has been sold for taxes thirteen times. There hasn't been a peach crop in this part of Georgia for two years. The wet spring killed the watermelons. Nobody around here has money enough to buy fertilizer; and land is so poor the corn crop failed, and there wasn't enough grass to support the rabbits. All the people have had to eat in this section for over a year is hog and hominy, and —"

"Pick," interrupts Caligula, mussing up his red hair, "what are you going to do with that chicken-feed?"

I hands the money back to Major Tucker; and then I goes over to Colonel Rockingham and slaps him on the back.

"Colonel," says I, "I hope you've enjoyed our little joke. We don't want to carry it too far. Kidnappers! Well, wouldn't it tickle your uncle? My name's Rhinegelder, and I'm a nephew of Chauncey Depew. My friend's a second cousin of the editor of *Puck*. So you can see. We are down South enjoying ourselves in our humorous way. Now, there's two quarts of cognac to open yet, and then the joke's over."

What's the use to go into details? One or two will

be enough. I remember Major Tallahassee Tucker playing on a jew's-harp, and Caligula waltzing with his head on the watch pocket of a tall baggage-master. I hesitate to refer to the cake-walk done by me and Mr. Patterson G. Coble with Colonel Jackson T. Rockingham between us.

And even on the next morning, when you wouldn't think it possible, there was a consolation for me and Caligula. We knew that Raisuli himself never made half the hit with Burdick Harris that we did with the Sunrise & Edenville Tap Railroad.

THE ETHICS OF PIG

On an east-bound train I went into the smoker and found Jefferson Peters, the only man with a brain west of the Wabash River who can use his cerebrum cerebellum, and medulla oblongata at the same time.

Jeff is in the line of unillegal graft. He is not to be dreaded by widows and orphans; he is a reducer of surplusage. His favorite disguise is that of the target-bird at which the spendthrift or the reckless investor may shy a few inconsequential dollars. He is readily vocalized by tobacco; so, with the aid of two thick and easy-burning brevas, I got the story of his latest Autolycan adventure.

"In my line of business," said Jeff, "the hardest thing is to find an upright, trustworthy, strictly honorable partner to work a graft with. Some of the best men I ever worked with in a swindle would resort to trickery at times.

"So, last summer, I thinks I will go over into this section of country where I hear the serpent has not

222

yet entered, and see if I can find a partner naturally gifted with a talent for crime, but not yet contaminated by success.

" I found a village that seemed to show the right kind of a layout. The inhabitants hadn't found out that Adam had been dispossessed, and were going right along naming the animals and killing snakes just as if they were in the Garden of Eden. They call this town Mount Nebo, and it's up near the spot where Kentucky and West Virginia and North Carolina corner together. Them States don't meet? Well, it was in that neighborhood, anyway.

" After putting in a week proving I wasn't a revenue officer, I went over to the store where the rude fourflushers of the hamlet lied, to see if I could get a line on the kind of man I wanted.

" ' Gentlemen,' says I, after we had rubbed noses and gathered 'round the dried-apple barrel. ' I don't suppose there's another community in the whole world into which sin and chicanery has less extensively permeated than this. Life here, where all the women are brave and propitious and all the men honest and expedient, must, indeed, be an idol. It reminds me,' says I, ' of Goldstein's beautiful ballad entitled " The Deserted Village," which says:

'Ill fares the land, to hastening ills a prey;
 What art can drive its charms away?
 The judge rode slowly down the lane, mother.
 For I'm to be Queen of the May.'

" 'Why, yes, Mr. Peters,' says the storekeeper.
'I reckon we air about as moral and torpid a community as there be on the mounting, according to
censuses of opinion; but I reckon you ain't ever met
Rufe Tatum.'

" 'Why, no,' says the town constable, ' he can't
hardly have ever.   That air Rufe is shore the monstrousest scalawag that has escaped hangin' on the
galluses.   And that puts me in mind that I ought to
have turned Rufe out of the lockup day before yesterday.   The thirty days he got for killin' Yance
Goodloe was up then.   A day or two more won't hurt
Rufe any, though.'

" 'Shucks, now,' says I, in the mountain idiom,
' don't tell me there's a man in Mount Nebo as bad
as that.'

" 'Worse,' says the storekeeper.   'He steals hogs.'

" I think I will look up this Mr. Tatum; so a day
or two after the constable turned him out I got acquainted with him and invited him out on the edge of
town to sit on a log and talk business.

" What I wanted was a partner with a natural

rural make-up to play a part in some little one-act outrages that I was going to book with the Pitfall & Gin circuit in some of the Western towns; and this R. Tatum was born for the rôle as sure as nature cast Fairbanks for the stuff that kept *Eliza* from sinking into the river.

"He was about the size of a first baseman; and he had ambiguous blue eyes like the china dog on the mantelpiece that Aunt Harriet used to play with when she was a child. His hair waved a little bit like the statue of the dinkus-thrower in the Vacation at Rome, but the color of it reminded you of the 'Sunset in the Grand Cañon, by an American Artist,' that they hang over the stove-pipe holes in the salongs. He was the Reub, without needing a touch. You'd have known him for one, even if you'd seen him on the vaudeville stage with one cotton suspender and a straw over his ear.

"I told him what I wanted, and found him ready to jump at the job.

"'Overlooking such a trivial little peccadillo as the habit of manslaughter,' says I, 'what have you accomplished in the way of indirect brigandage or non-actionable thriftiness that you could point to, with or without pride, as an evidence of your qualifications for the position?'

" ' Why,' says he, in his kind of Southern system of procrastinated accents, ' hain't you heard tell? There ain't any man, black or white, in the Blue Ridge that can tote off a shoat as easy as I can without bein' heard, seen, or cotched. I can lift a shoat,' he goes on, ' out of a pen, from under a porch, at the trough, in the woods, day or night, anywhere or anyhow, and I guarantee nobody won't hear a squeal. It's all in the way you grab hold of 'em and carry 'em atterwards. Some day,' goes on this gentle despoiler of pig-pens, ' I hope to become reckernized as the champion shoat-stealer of the world.'

" ' It's proper to be ambitious,' says I; ' and hog-stealing will do very well for Mount Nebo; but in the outside world, Mr. Tatum, it would be considered as crude a piece of business as a bear raid on Bay State Gas. However, it will do as a guarantee of good faith. We'll go into partnership. I've got a thousand dollars cash capital; and with that homeward-plods atmosphere of yours we ought to be able to win out a few shares of Soon Parted, preferred, in the money market.'

" So I attaches Rufe, and we go away from Mount Nebo down into the lowlands. And all the way I coach him for his part in the grafts I had in mind. I had idled away two months on the Florida coast, and was feeling all to the Ponce de Leon, besides having so many new schemes up my sleeve that I had to wear kimonos to hold 'em.

" I intended to assume a funnel shape and mow a path nine miles wide through the farming belt of the Middle West; so we headed in that direction. But when we got as far as Lexington we found Binkley Brothers' circus there, and the blue-grass peasantry romping into town and pounding the Belgian blocks with their hand-pegged sabots as artless and arbitrary as an extra session of a Datto Bryan duma. I never pass a circus without pulling the valve-cord and coming down for a little Key West money; so I engaged a couple of rooms and board for Rufe and me at a house near the circus grounds run by a widow lady named Peevy. Then I took Rufe to a clothing store and gent's-outfitted him. He showed up strong, as I knew he would, after he was rigged up in the ready-made rutabaga regalia. Me and old Misfitzky stuffed him into a bright blue suit with a Nile green visible plaid effect, and riveted on a fancy vest of a light Tuskegee Normal tan color, a red necktie, and the yellowest pair of shoes in town.

They were the first clothes Rufe had ever worn except the gingham layette and the butternut top-dressing of his native kraal, and he looked as self-conscious of an Igorrote with a new nose-ring.

"That night I went down to the circus tents and opened a small shell game. Rufe was to be the capper. I gave him a roll of phony currency to bet with and kept a bunch of it in a special pocket to pay his winnings out of. No; I didn't mistrust him; but I simply can't manipulate the ball to lose when I see real money bet. My fingers go on a strike every time I try it.

"I set up my little table and began to show them how easy it was to guess which shell the little pea was under. The unlettered hinds gathered in a thick semicircle and began to nudge elbows and banter one another to bet. Then was when Rufe ought to have single-footed up and called the turn on the little joker for a few tens and fives to get them started. But, no Rufe. I'd seen him two or three times walking about and looking at the side-show pictures with his mouth full of peanut candy; but he never came nigh.

"The crowd piked a little; but trying to work the shells without a capper is like fishing without bait. I closed the game with only forty-two dollars of the unearned increment, while I had been counting on yanking the yeomen for two hundred at least. I went home at eleven and went to bed. I supposed that the circus had proved too alluring for Rufe, and that he had succumbed to it, concert and all; but I meant to give him a lecture on general business principles in the morning.

" Just after Morpheus had got both my shoulders to the shuck mattress I hears a houseful of unbecoming and ribald noises like a youngster screeching with green-apple colic. I opens my door and calls out in the hall for the widow lady, and when she sticks her head out, I says: ' Mrs. Peevy, ma'am, would you mind choking off that kid of yours so that honest people can get their rest? '

" ' Sir,' says she, ' it's no child of mine. It's the pig squealing that your friend Mr. Tatum brought home to his room a couple of hours ago. And if you are uncle or second cousin or brother to it, I'd appreciate your stopping its mouth, sir, yourself, if you please.'

" I put on some of the polite outside habiliments of external society and went into Rufe's room. He had gotten up and lit his lamp, and was pouring some milk into a tin pan on the floor for a dingy-white, half-grown, squealing pig.

" ' How is this, Rufe? ' says I. ' You flimflammed in your part of the work to-night and put the game on crutches. And how do you explain the pig? It looks like back-sliding to me.'

"'Now, don't be too hard on me, Jeff,' says he. 'You know how long I've been used to stealing shoats. It's got to be a habit with me. And to-night, when I see such a fine chance, I couldn't help takin' it.'

"'Well,' says I, 'maybe you've really got kleptopigia. And maybe when we get out of the pig belt you'll turn your mind to higher and more remunerative misconduct. Why you should want to stain your soul with such a distasteful, feeble-minded, perverted, roaring beast as that I can't understand.'

"'Why, Jeff,' says he, 'you ain't in sympathy with shoats. You don't understand 'em like I do. This here seems to me to be an animal of more than common powers of ration and intelligence. He walked half across the room on his hind legs a while ago.'

"'Well, I'm going back to bed,' says I. 'See if you can impress it upon your friend's ideas of intelligence that he's not to make so much noise.'

"'He was hungry,' says Rufe. 'He'll go to sleep and keep quiet now.'

"I always get up before breakfast and read the morning paper whenever I happen to be within the radius of a Hoe cylinder or a Washington hand-press.

The next morning I got up early, and found a Lexington daily on the front porch where the carrier had thrown it. The first thing I saw in it was a double-column ad. on the front page that read like this:

FIVE THOUSAND DOLLARS REWARD

The above amount will be paid, and no questions asked, for the return, alive and uninjured, of Beppo, the famous European educated pig, that strayed or was stolen from the side-show tents of Binkley Bros.' circus last night.

GEO. B. TAPLEY, Business Manager.

At the circus grounds.

" I folded up the paper flat, put it into my inside pocket, and went to Rufe's room. He was nearly dressed, and was feeding the pig the rest of the milk and some apple-peelings.

" ' Well, well, well, good morning all,' I says, hearty and amiable. ' So we are up? And piggy is having his breakfast. What had you intended doing with that pig, Rufe? '

" ' I'm going to crate him up,' says Rufe, ' and express him to ma in Mount Nebo. He'll be company for her while I am away.'

" ' He's a mighty fine pig,' says I, scratching him on the back.

" ' You called him a lot of names last night,' says Rufe

" ' Oh, well,' says I, ' he looks better to me this morning. I was raised on a farm, and I'm very fond of pigs. I used to go to bed at sundown, so I never saw one by lamplight before. Tell you what I'll do, Rufe,' I says. ' I'll give you ten dollars for that pig.'

" ' I reckon I wouldn't sell this shoat,' says he. ' If it was any other one I might.'

" ' Why not this one? ' I asked, fearful that he might know something.

" ' Why, because,' says he, ' it was the grandest achievement of my life. There ain't airy other man that could have done it. If I ever have a fireside and children, I'll sit beside it and tell 'em how their daddy toted off a shoat from a whole circus full of people. And maybe my grandchildren, too. They'll certainly be proud a whole passel. Why,' says he, ' there was two tents, one openin' into the other. This shoat was on a platform, tied with a little chain. I seen a giant and a lady with a fine chance of bushy white hair in the other tent. I got the shoat and crawled out from under the canvas again without him squeakin' as loud as a mouse. I put him under my coat, and I must have passed a hundred folks before I got out where the streets was dark. I reckon I wouldn't sell that shoat, Jeff. I'd want ma to keep it, so there'd be a witness to what I done.'

" ' The pig won't live long enough,' I says, ' to use as an exhibit in your senile fireside mendacity. Your grandchildren will have to take your word for it. I'll give you one hundred dollars for the animal.'

" Rufe looked at me astonished.

" ' The shoat can't be worth anything like that to you,' he says. ' What do you want him for? '

" ' Viewing me casuistically,' says I, with a rare smile, ' you wouldn't think that I've got an artistic side to my temper. But I have. I'm a collector of pigs. I've scoured the world for unusual pigs. Over in the Wabash Valley I've got a hog ranch with most every specimen on it, from a Merino to a Poland China. This looks like a blooded pig to me, Rufe,' says I. ' I believe it's a genuine Berkshire. That's why I'd like to have it.'

" ' I'd shore like to accommodate you,' says he, ' but I've got the artistic tenement, too. I don't see why it ain't art when you can steal a shoat better than anybody else can. Shoats is a kind of inspiration and genius with me. Specially this one. I wouldn't take two hundred and fifty for that animal.'

" ' Now, listen,' says I, wiping off my forehead.

'It's not so much a matter of business with me as it is art; and not so much art as it is philanthropy. Being a connoisseur and disseminator of pigs, I wouldn't feel like I'd done my duty to the world unless I added that Berkshire to my collection. Not intrinsically, but according to the ethics of pigs as friends and coadjutors of mankind, I offer you five hundred dollars for the animal.'

"'Jeff,' says this pork esthete, 'it ain't money; it's sentiment with me.'

"'Seven hundred,' says I.

"'Make it eight hundred,' says Rufe, 'and I'll crush the sentiment out of my heart.'

"I went under my clothes for my money-belt, and counted him out forty twenty-dollar gold certificates.

"'I'll just take him into my own room,' says I, 'and lock him up till after breakfast.'

"I took the pig by the hind leg. He turned on a squeal like the steam calliope at the circus.

"'Let me tote him in for you,' says Rufe; and he picks up the beast under one arm, holding his snout with the other hand, and packs him into my room like a sleeping baby.

"After breakfast Rufe, who had a chronic case of haberdashery ever since I got his trousseau, says he believes he will amble down to Misfitzky's and look over some royal-purple socks. And then I got as busy as a one-armed man with the nettle-rash pasting on wall-paper. I found an old negro man with an express wagon to hire; and we tied the pig in a sack and drove down to the circus grounds.

" I found George B. Tapley in a little tent with a window flap open. He was a fattish man with an immediate eye, in a black skull-cap, with a four-ounce diamond screwed into the bosom of his red sweater.

" ' Are you George B. Tapley? ' I asks.

" ' I swear it,' says he.

" ' Well, I've got it,' says I.

" ' Designate,' says he. ' Are you the guinea pigs for the Asiatic python or the alfalfa for the sacred buffalo? '

" ' Neither,' says I. ' I've got Beppo, the educated hog, in a sack in that wagon. I found him rooting up the flowers in my front yard this morning. I'll take the five thousand dollars in large bills, if it's handy.'

" George B. hustles out of his tent, and asks me to follow. We went into one of the side-shows. In there was a jet black pig with a pink ribbon around his neck lying on some hay and eating carrots that a man was feeding to him.

" 'Hey, Mac,' calls G. B. 'Nothing wrong with the world-wide this morning, is there?'

" 'Him? No,' says the man. 'He's got an appetite like a chorus girl at 1 A. M.'

" 'How'd you get this pipe?' says Tapley to me. 'Eating too many pork chops last night?'

" I pulls out the paper and shows him the ad.

" 'Fake,' says he. 'Don't know anything about it. You've beheld with your own eyes the marvelous, world-wide porcine wonder of the four-footed kingdom eating with preternatural sagacity his matutinal meal, unstrayed and unstole. Good morning.'

" I was beginning to see. I got in the wagon and told Uncle Ned to drive to the most adjacent orifice of the nearest alley. There I took out my pig, got the range carefully for the other opening, set his sights, and gave him such a kick that he went out the other end of the alley twenty feet ahead of his squeal.

" Then I paid Uncle Ned his fifty cents, and walked down to the newspaper office. I wanted to hear it in cold syllables. I got the advertising man to his window.

" 'To decide a bet,' says I, 'wasn't the man who had this ad. put in last night short and fat, with long, black whiskers and a club-foot?'

" 'He was not,' says the man. 'He would measure

about six feet by four and a half inches, with corn-silk hair, and dressed like the pansies of the conservatory.'

" At dinner time I went back to Mrs. Peevy's.

" ' Shall I keep some soup hot for Mr. Tatum till he comes back? ' she asks.

" ' If you do, ma'am,' says I, ' you'll more than exhaust for firewood all the coal in the bosom of the earth and all the forests on the outside of it.'

" So there, you see," said Jefferson Peters, in conclusion, " how hard it is ever to find a fair-minded and honest business-partner."

" But," I began, with the freedom of long acquaintance, " the rule should work both ways. If you had offered to divide the reward you would not have lost —"

Jeff's look of dignified reproach stopped me.

" That don't involve the same principles at all," said he. " Mine was a legitimate and moral attempt at speculation. Buy low and sell high — don't Wall street indorse it? Bulls and bears and pigs — what's the difference? Why not bristles as well as horns and fur? "

THE END

THE COUNTRY LIFE PRESS
GARDEN CITY, N. Y.

DATE DUE			
OCT 31 '88			
Nov 28			